D1326074

Flame Across the Land

Fark Seaton comes to the aid of old timer Utah Red when he and his flock of sheep are attacked. Who is responsible? The evidence seems to point towards Mitch Montgomery and his Lazy Ladder outfit, but as tension mounts and the bullets fly, Seaton is not so sure. What is the role of Nash Brandon, owner of the Mill Iron? Could Seaton's interest in Montgomery's daughter, Maisie, be clouding his judgement?

Fark and Utah go undercover to solve the mystery. When the sparks of anger finally blaze into uncontrolled fury, the answers at last begin to emerge.

Flame Across the Land

Colin Bainbridge

A Black Horse Western

ROBERT HALE

ISBN 978-0-7198-2039-7

The Crowood Press
The Stable Block
Crowood Lane
Ramsbury
Marlborough
Wiltshire SN8 2HR

www.crowood.com

Robert Hale is an imprint
of The Crowood Press

Typeset by
Derek Doyle & Associates, Shaw Heath
Printed and bound in Great Britain by
CPI Group (UK) Ltd, Croydon, CR0 4YY

CHAPTER ONE

Fark Seaton was bent down in the water panning when he saw the oldster coming down the trail, riding on a brown-and-white pinto. He stood up to his full six feet and watched as he approached.

'Well I'll be a goddamn polecat,' he muttered. 'If it ain't old Utah Red.' The oldster stopped and dismounted, a little stiffly.

'Howdy, Utah,' Seaton remarked. 'I sure didn't expect to see you again for a whiles.'

The old timer stroked the skewbald's head. 'Me neither,' he replied. 'I figured you'd be gone by this time.'

'You ain't far wrong. I've just about decided this prospectin' ain't any kind of a life,' Seaton said. He splashed out of the stream. 'Who's taking care of those sheep?' he added.

'The company was supposed to be keepin' me in supplies but I ain't seen anyone. In the end I figured, if I needed supplies, I'd have to go and get them myself.' Utah paused, looking at Seaton with a quizzical expression.

'It's a ways to go to town,' Seaton said. He threw the pan he was holding to one side. 'I reckon you could probably use some coffee.'

'I sure could,' the oldster responded.

They walked across to where Seaton's tent stood by a clump of willows. The embers of a fire were still smouldering and it took no time at all for Seaton to build it up again and replace the tripod from which he hung a battered kettle. When the coffee was ready he filled two tin cups with the thick black liquid. The oldster was about to take his first sip when Seaton produced a worn flask.

'Somethin' to stiffen it up a little,' he said. They sat quietly for a while, savouring the coffee, till Seaton spoke again.

'That leg of yours seems to have got worse since last time I saw you,' he said.

Utah glanced down at his leg and stroked it with his hand.

'I guess I'm just gettin' older,' he said.

'How did you come by it anyway?'

'It's a legacy from the war. Not the last one, you understand. The one in Mexico. But it ain't nothin' much.' He took another swallow.

'Anyhow,' he continued, 'it don't come as any surprise to me to find you ain't found nothin'. I told you the whole place is worked out. I tried that game myself – more than once. The way I figure it, there was never anythin' here in the first place.'

6

Seaton didn't reply but instead got to his feet and went inside the tent, reappearing after a few moments with a leather pouch tied with a drawstring. Opening it, he handed it to the oldster.

'Go on, take a look,' he said.

Utah peered inside. 'Holy cow!' he exclaimed. 'You have struck lucky!'

'I don't know what it's worth. Maybe not much. Either way, I ain't concerned. Take it if you like.'

Utah looked at him disbelievingly and then shook his head as he handed the gold dust back. 'Thanks,' he said, 'but that's yours.' He raised his head and glanced towards the tent. 'Howsomever,' he continued, 'you could sure do me a big favour.'

Seaton smiled. 'I've got supplies,' he said. 'You're welcome to take what you need.'

'I'd sure appreciate that. I won't take much. Just enough to see me through till the supply wagon comes through.'

'How do you know it is comin'? After all, it ain't appeared yet.'

'It'll come,' Utah replied. 'I guess it just got delayed somehow.'

They finished their mugs of coffee and Seaton refilled them. 'What did you say was the name of the company you're workin' for?' he asked.

'You know, I ain't rightly sure. They operate out of a building in Lindenberg.'

'And how long are you contracted for?'

'Spring and summer. Six months.'

Seaton thought for a moment, calculating from

the last time he had seen the oldster. 'You're not halfway through yet,' he said.

'I don't know. I guess not. A man kinda loses track of time up in those hills.' They continued talking for a while till the coffee was finished and then Utah got to his feet.

'OK if I take a look and borrow some of those supplies?' he asked.

'Go right on ahead. Take what you need. In fact, take the lot.'

'I couldn't do that,' the oldster replied.

'You'd be doin' me a favour,' Seaton said.

'But what will you do?'

'Like I say, I've had about enough of prospectin'.'

'You can't give up now.'

'Nope. I've given it a try and it ain't for me. Tell you what. When you've finished lookin' after those sheep, why don't you take over my claim?'

The oldster's face creased in a snaggle-toothed grin. 'It's a nice offer,' he said, 'but I'm gettin' too old for that game.'

'It can't be harder than herdin' sheep.'

'Sheep are alive. There's a big difference.'

Seaton didn't argue the point. When Utah had taken what he needed he helped him load the supplies on the skewbald.

'I owe you,' the oldster said. He climbed awkwardly into the saddle and shook hands with Seaton.

'Mind how you go,' Seaton said.

'I guess I can take care of myself after all these years,' Utah replied. Seaton looked him in the face.

'Yeah, maybe so,' he said.

Utah spoke some words to the horse and it began to amble forward. Seaton watched as the pinto climbed slowly up the trail until eventually it disappeared from view. Then he bent down and picked up his pan and was about to step back into the stream when he uttered a low oath and flung the pan away again, this time into the water. He stepped up on to the bank and made his way back to his tent. In no time at all he had dismantled it and removed all traces of ever having been there. He stood for a while, looking around and wondering what to do with his equipment. It didn't amount to much but he didn't see much point in lugging it back to town. In the end he ploughed back into the water to retrieve his pan. Adding it to the rest of his gear, he wrapped it in the tent and stacked it beneath an overhang of the stream bank. Then he saddled up his horse, which was tethered at a little distance, and stepped into the leather. His days as a prospector were over.

He made camp that night and rode the chestnut mare into Lindenberg late the following morning. He left the horse at the livery stable, booked a room for a couple of nights at the Exchange Hotel and then made his way to the barber shop. The place was empty and he took a seat as the barber stropped his razor.

'Passin' through?' the barber remarked.

'Yeah.'

The barber began to lather his face. 'I don't know what your plans are,' he said, 'but if it's work you're

9

lookin' for, there are jobs to be had at Nash Brandon's spread.'

'Nash Brandon?'

The man paused for a moment in his ministrations.

'I can see you must be a stranger round these parts if you ain't heard of Nash Brandon,' he said. 'Hell, he's the biggest ranch-owner in the county. Owns a place called the Mill Iron not too far out of town. Likes to ride a big palomino.'

'Thanks for the tip. I'll bear it in mind.'

'Rumour has it he intends runnin' for mayor. I'd say that was only the start of it. The way I see it, it's his for the askin'. Hell, he'll be aimin' for the Senate before too long. He's very influential with the Cattle Ranch and Land Company, and that goes a long way.' The barber stopped long enough to draw the razor along Seaton's chin-line before resuming.

'Some folks say it'd be a good thing for the town. Me, I ain't so sure.'

Whether he intended elaborating on the theme Seaton was not to know, because just at that juncture the bell above the outer door jangled and another customer came in. After he had greeted the newcomer, the barber continued talking but it was of a more desultory nature, and Seaton was not inclined to make conversation. It was a relief when the barber had finished and he stepped back out into the sunlight, cropped and clean-shaven. Leaning against a stanchion, he took the opportunity to observe the town.

It was much like others he had seen or spent time in, with one main street lined with false-fronted buildings. It was not long after midday and the place had a sleepy look. Not many people moved about and the awnings were pulled down over those stores that had one. A few tethered horses flicked lazily at flies with their tails; a one-horse buggy was standing outside the millinery shop and a freight wagon stood outside the main emporium with its ox team lying under their yokes in the dust. Seaton suddenly felt thirsty. There were several saloons lining the main drag and, selecting the nearest one, the Blue Front, he stepped down from the boardwalk and began to walk towards it.

He hadn't gone far when the peace was suddenly shattered by gunshots and whooping and a trio of horsemen appeared at a junction further along. They were firing their six-guns randomly into the air but that didn't prevent a stray bullet from shattering the upstairs window of a building. Seaton's instant reaction was to draw his own gun as he flung himself sideways in order to get out of the way of the oncoming horsemen, taking shelter behind a water trough. The riders swept by, finally drawing their mounts almost to their haunches outside the Blue Front where they dismounted and tied the horses to the hitch-rack. Raising their weapons, they fired a few more rounds into the sky before finally placing them back in their holsters and crashing their way into the saloon.

Seaton got to his feet, moved quickly across to

11

their tethered horses and bent down to see if they carried any markings. For some reason it came as no surprise to him to see that they carried a Mill Iron brand. Sounds of loud, raucous laughter were spilling from the saloon and he was about to step inside when he heard a commotion and looked up to see a trio of people milling about outside the grocery store. The buggy was still there but it was standing at a crazy angle and sideways to the street. He quickly realized that the horse must have been skittered by the gunshots and reared up in the traces. The group consisted of an elderly woman and a man who was gesticulating and who was obviously the shopkeeper. It was the third person, however, who arrested his attention.

She looked about twenty and was wearing a checked gingham dress, which did nothing to hide her figure. For a moment he hesitated and then made his way across. The young woman was standing quietly while the shopkeeper fussed and the older woman shouted frantically.

'Where's the marshal? Where's Marshal Braithwaite?'

Taking control of the situation, he calmed the horse before pulling the buggy straight and upright again with a heave of his muscles. When he had done so, he turned to the young woman and raised his Stetson.

'It's OK,' he said, 'no real harm done.'

The woman looked up at him and smiled.

'How did you know it was my buggy?' she said in a

lilting tone.

'Just an educated guess,' he replied.

She gave him a look which he couldn't interpret and then turned to the shopkeeper.

'Could you have my purchases brought out and placed in the buggy?' she said.

'Of course. Right away, Miss Maisie,' he replied.

The older woman had ceased calling for the marshal and instead was intoning against the recklessness of the riders whose noise had scared the horse.

'It's about time somethin' was done,' she said. 'One of these days it'll be somethin' more serious.'

Seaton looked across the street towards the Blue Front saloon. 'Probably just a few youngsters lettin' off steam,' he said. 'Still, I reckon someone ought to have a word with 'em.'

'They need more than that. They need dealin' with.'

Seaton turned to her. 'As a matter of fact, where is the marshal?' he asked.

'Don't ask me. All I know is that he never seems to be there when he's needed.'

Seaton glanced again towards the saloon. The shouts and laughter that had been emanating from it seemed to have temporarily subsided. He was about to take a step in its direction when he was halted by the voice of the younger woman.

'I'd leave it,' she remarked. 'As you said, no real harm has been done and things seem to have quieted down.'

Seaton felt he had a personal score to settle with the rowdies and his inclination was to go across to the saloon and confront them, but he saw the sense in what the young woman was saying. There was a possibility that things might boil over and he certainly didn't want to take the risk of involving her in anything. Just at that instant the shopkeeper appeared, followed by a freckle-faced, jug-eared boy of about ten, each carrying a pile of foodstuffs which they began to place carefully in the buggy.

'Thank you, Mr Candless,' the woman said, 'and you too, Andy.' From somewhere she produced a coin, which she pressed into the boy's hand. Then she turned to Seaton.

'Thank you, too,' she said. Seaton didn't know what to reply and instead put out a hand to help her up into the buggy. When she was seated he had a sudden inspiration.

'If you need any assistance,' he began to mutter, 'I don't know . . . maybe I could. . . .'

'It's all right, Mr . . .' She paused in turn.

'Seaton,' he added.

'It's all right, Mr Seaton. I'm quite recovered from the shock. Besides, I haven't far to go.'

'If you're quite sure, ma'am.'

She looked at him and gave another smile, then raised the whip and flicked it over the horse's head. The buggy began to roll down the street, raising a thin cloud of dust. Seaton wasn't aware he was watching it till the voice of the old lady cut in.

'Don't worry,' she said. 'Miss Montgomery will be

perfectly safe. She can look after herself as well as anyone. She's a regular visitor to town; not to the clothing store or Johnson's Millinery, as you might expect, but always to stock up on groceries and supplies.'

'Does she live in Lindenberg?'

'Just out of town. Her father owns the Lazy Ladder. She was born and bred there. I knew her mother.'

'Are you sure you'll be OK?' Seaton asked.

'Thank you for asking, young man,' she said. 'I'll be fine.'

The shopkeeper and the boy had gone back inside. There seemed to be nothing else to do except say his goodbye, so raising his hat again and mumbling a few words he turned and began to make his way back in the direction of the hotel. As he passed the saloon, he halted for a few moments, deliberating whether to go inside. In the normal course of events he wouldn't have hesitated, but something held him back; it was a vague feeling almost of loyalty, as if he owed it to the young woman to do as she had suggested and let it ride. He didn't understand it, but it was enough for him to carry on walking.

He spent the next couple of days hanging about town, some of it in the Blue Front saloon, but he saw no sign of the riders from the Mill Iron. He got into the habit of taking his meals at an eating house with the grandiose title of the Broadway Coffee Shop and called by the livery stables several times to check on his horse. He would have gone to the Assay Office but that particular establishment was defunct, from which he deduced that he had indeed been lucky in finding any traces of gold and that it was unlikely he would have found much more even if he had stayed. He did some shopping for new duds and was solicited more than once, gently turning down the offers. His hotel room had a small balcony from which he got some pleasure watching the activities in the street below but by the evening of the second day he had had enough. He was bored, and even the possibility of seeing Maisie Montgomery again was not enough to persuade him to stay any longer.

As he lay on his bed that night, looking up at the ceiling and blowing smoke rings in the air into the early hours of the morning, he found himself thinking of old Utah Red. He had an image of the oldster riding away on the skewbald, making his lone way into the hills where his sheep would be lost without their shepherd. Utah probably imagined he had a good, respected job, but Seaton knew that wasn't the case. This was cow country and sheepmen were held in very low regard. That was probably why he had been taken on in the first place: because no one else would do it. Cattlemen hated sheep. As far as the ranchers were concerned, sheep ruined the land. They didn't graze like cattle did, but cropped it down to the roots, or so they claimed. So what did that signify with regard to the oldster? Thinking about the situation, Seaton began to grow more and more concerned. Given the way things were, the oldster had put himself in the way of danger, returning to his solitary vigil. As dawn began to break, Seaton realized what he must do. Arriving at the livery stable as soon as it was open, he saddled the chestnut, placed his Winchester in its scabbard, and rode out to look for the old man.

He didn't know exactly where the oldster was to be found, except that he was somewhere in the hills. The obvious thing to do was to begin the search at the point where he had last seen Utah, which was his own camp by the stream. It was late in the afternoon when he got there. He had done a good job of clearing the site. A passing traveller would never have realized anyone had been there. He was tempted to set up camp on the same spot but decided to carry on further. When he had gone a little way beyond where he had seen the last of the oldster, he got down from his horse and examined the ground for traces of the skewbald's sign and saw enough to make him think he had found it. However, he couldn't be sure. Tracking wasn't one of his strong points and other people had passed through. There were animal tracks too. He decided that the best thing would be to follow the lie of the land. Any trail would follow the line of least resistance and he would carry on that way until he saw good reason to turn aside.

He climbed back into leather and carried on riding while the sun sank lower in the sky till eventually it was a fading yellow ball poised just above the line of the western hills. At that point he decided to call a halt. As the shadows descended, he first tended to the horse and then built a fire. He laid slabs of bacon in the skillet and made coffee with water from a nearby run-off. By the time he had eaten, darkness had fallen. A cool wind blew down from the ranges and from somewhere a bird called. The sky wheeled with stars and he could see for quite a distance into the luminous night. He was glad to have left the town behind, but that didn't prevent him from feeling a touch lonesome. He thought about old Utah, spending night after night in some remote valley with only his sheep for company, and felt a twinge of regret that he hadn't done more to help him. But what could he have done? Then he remembered the oldster's limp. Was Utah's account of it quite accurate? Whether it was or not, he had justification for feeling concern. When he finally turned in it was with a renewed purpose to locate the oldster as quickly as he could.

Dawn came up and he quickly made breakfast before climbing into the saddle and setting out again. As he got further into the hills, the trail became less easy to follow. It was barely discernible; an old Indian track abandoned by them long since. There were wildflowers and scattered stands of aspen and spruce lining the hillsides. When he dismounted to search for signs, he could find nothing but animal tracks and presently he came upon the deer which had made them, about a dozen of them standing in a bunch. He saw marmots and at one point an eagle came swooping down and flew overhead for some time before soaring away over the crest of a ridge.

As time went by, he began to be less certain that he

18

was on the right track, but there was nothing else to do but carry on and keep watch for any indication of the oldster's whereabouts. Despite his concerns, he took pleasure in observing the scenery, in savouring the clean air and the fresh, aromatic smell of the grass and the trees, things which he realized he had been missing too long. Maybe that was the real reason the oldster sought out the lonely, wide-open spaces and spent his time there. The trail was growing steep as it followed the shoulder of a tree-lined peak. Then it took a turn and he found himself on a grassy slope that fell away quite sharply into a secluded valley ringed with high hills, beyond which stood ragged peaks with escarpments of steep rock. Far below, he could see patches of white and when he took a closer look through his field-glasses, he could see that they were sheep. The only trouble was that some of them weren't moving. He had found the place he was looking for, but if some of the sheep were dead, in what state would he find the old man? It was apparent already that all was not as it should be. Touching the mare's flanks with his spurs, as quickly as he dared, he began the descent.

The hillside was comparatively steep, and he had to go carefully, but eventually the chestnut reached the valley floor. As he moved on, he began to see sheep in little bunches, scattered about the grassy meadows. He considered trying to herd them but decided against it. It would take up time and he was anxious to reach the oldster. He spurred the horse and it broke into a trot, hoofs drumming gently on the soft earth, and soon, topping a rise, he saw what looked like Utah's camp a little way ahead of him.

There were various items of equipment scattered about the remains of a fire and a tattered tent lay ripped and torn nearby, but there was no sign of Utah. As he rode up he called the oldster's name without eliciting a response. He leaped from the horse and began looking around. It didn't take long. He was in something of a quandary as to what he should do when he suddenly heard a dog bark. Getting back on board the chestnut, he began to ride in the direction from which the sound seemed to come. It came again and then he saw, some way off to his right, the figure of the oldster. He had two dogs with him, and together they were attempting to herd a bunch of sheep. Utah had obviously seen him too, because he stopped and looked towards him, shielding his eyes against the sun. Seaton waved and called out his name and it seemed the oldster finally recognized him. Seaton dismounted and walked the rest of the distance between them, not wanting to scare the sheep. As he approached, one of the dogs ran up and began to jump up at him. He took its head between his hands and stroked its fur, but at a call from Utah it dropped down and returned to its position.

'Looks like Jasper's taken to you,' the oldster said as Seaton came up to him.

'And there was I thinkin' you were all alone,' Seaton replied.

'A man ain't ever alone when he's got a good dog for company.' Utah paused before attempting a smile. 'Hell,' he said. 'Am I glad to see you. But what in tarnation are you doin' here?'

Seaton looked closely at the old man. Utah seemed to be OK, but he couldn't be certain. Something had happened for sure but he would have to wait for an explanation.

'Let me help you faze these critters back to wherever you want 'em,' Seaton said. 'After that we can get down to talkin'.'

Utah didn't object and, taking his cue from the oldster, Seaton took his place at the side of the flock, trying to keep it tight and prevent strays from breaking away. They were making slow progress back towards the camp and the oldster had no objection to Seaton getting back on his horse as they passed it. The chestnut seemed, if anything, more nervous than the sheep. It wasn't an easy task. Every now and then the sheep would begin to run in little spurts but the dogs, under Utah's control, kept them from going too far and finally they were left to graze on a grassy stretch leading from the camp towards the foot of the nearest hill. That wasn't the end of the matter, however, because the oldster insisted on rounding up the rest of the flock while it was still light.

'I got most of 'em,' he said, 'but there are still some wanderin' out there.'

'I know,' Seaton answered. 'I saw a few of 'em.'

He didn't mention the dead sheep he had seen. By the time they had rounded up the live ones, it was late and they were tired. While the oldster set about building up the ashes of his fire, Seaton attended the chestnut until eventually, as the evening shadows deepened, they were able to sit down together to eat. When they had finished, Seaton produced his pouch of Bull Durham and they built cigarettes.

'OK,' Seaton said. 'Tell me what happened.'

The oldster inhaled deeply and blew out a cloud of smoke. 'There ain't much to tell. There were three of 'em. They came ridin' in early this mornin'. I heard the shootin' first and managed to scramble out of the tent before they came chargin' through the camp.'

'Did you recognize 'em?'

'Nope. They could have been anybody. Your guess is as good as mine.'

'Well, it's a pretty safe bet they're connected to some cattle outfit. They're the only ones likely to be upset enough by the prospect of havin' sheep around to do somethin' like this.'

'This is free grass. They got no right.'

Seaton laughed. 'You think they're gonna worry about a little detail like that? Believe me, you're not the first to suffer this kind of treatment. I've come across it before. Men have been killed. If anythin', you can count yourself lucky you heard 'em comin'.'

'They killed some of my sheep,' Utah commented.

'Now you've been visited by these varmints, whoever they are,' Seaton replied, 'they might feel inclined to pay a return call. If I were you, I'd take the warnin'. Next time you might not be so lucky.'

The oldster gathered a ball of spit and jettisoned it

into the fire.

'They killed my sheep,' he said, 'and I got a con-tract till the end of the summer.'

Again Seaton laughed grimly. 'I wouldn't set a lot of store by that contract,' he said. 'I seem to remem-ber you havin' to seek out your own supplies because no one from the association bothered to turn up.'

'Maybe the association ain't been observin' the terms of the agreement, but that don't mean I won't.'

They sat back for a while talking and smoking in a desultory fashion while the fire burned down. Seaton was thinking about what the oldster had said. It was obvious he didn't fully realize the danger he was in. Besides that, he was a stubborn old coot. Seaton couldn't think of the right words to make him under-stand the situation. Finally he made one last appeal.

'Listen,' he said. 'The way I see it, the best thing you can do would be to pack that old paint and get out of here just as soon as you can.'

'I got some buryin' to do,' Utah replied somewhat inconsequentially. For a moment Seaton didn't realize he was talking about the sheep that had been shot.

'Think about it,' he said. 'If you're so concerned, take the sheep right along with you. But don't wait around here. Take them just as far away as you can.'

'I don't think the association would appreciate that.'

Seaton got to his feet in exasperation. 'If I had any sense, I'd saddle up that chestnut and leave right now myself,' he said.

The oldster looked up at him. 'You don't mean that,' he said.

'There's just one thing that's stoppin' me,' Seaton replied.

'Yeah? What's that?'

'There's a job that needs doin'.'

The oldster continued looking at him with a puzzled expression on his grizzled features.

'Helpin' to bury some sheep,' Seaton said.

CHAPTER TWO

Nash Brandon heard the sound of hoofs on the dry packed ground of the yard and looked out of the ranch-house window. Three men rode up and dismounted, and while two of them led the horses away in the direction of the stables, the other one climbed the steps to the veranda and knocked on the door.

'Come right on in!' Brandon shouted and in a moment the door opened and his foreman, Cooley Held, a thin short man dressed in black, entered. He was dusty from riding.

'I guess you could use a drink,' Brandon said. He walked over to a cabinet from which he produced a bottle and a couple of glasses.

'Don't stand on ceremony,' he said, 'take a seat.' He filled the glasses, handed one to Held and sat down himself in a large leather armchair. For a moment neither spoke as they drank the whisky.

'Fine Scotch,' Brandon remarked. 'Special import.'

'Sure tastes good,' Held said.

'I think you'll find it hits the spot.' Brandon took another sip. 'Well,' he said, 'How did it go?'

'We did just like you said,' Held replied.

'You didn't give the old goat too big a beatin'?'

'Nope, just enough to convince him he'd do best to get out.' Held uttered a sneering laugh. 'He'll have less of those sheep to move on when he does.'

Brandon smiled. 'Well, let's hope he gets the message.'

Held swallowed the last of his whisky and glanced at his boss. 'Why are we pussy-footin' with the old man?' he said. 'We coulda dealt with him and his goddamned sheep once and for all.'

Brandon shook his head and gave him a look of distaste. 'That might be necessary as a last resort,' he said, 'but we don't want to arouse any interest on the part of the federal authorities. I can keep the town marshal sweet, but there's nothing to be gained by drawing attention to ourselves. I always find that it pays to exercise a little discretion.'

'Unless it don't work,' Held replied.

Brandon glanced at him again. 'Yes, exactly,' he replied. 'Which reminds me; I may need you and the boys to help me apply a little more pressure on the Lazy Ladder.'

'They turned down your latest offer?'

'That would seem to be the case. I'll be seeing Snape tomorrow, but I don't see that two-bit lawyer offerin' anythin' new. He ain't done much so far. Anyway, I'll get back to you afterwards.' Brandon's heavy jowls tightened as he attempted a smile. 'And don't worry,' he added. 'I think the time's about come to stop bein' discreet, at least as far as Mitch Montgomery is concerned.'

Held, realizing that the interview was at an end, got to his feet and moved to the door. 'Anythin' you want, just let us know,' he said.

When he had left, Brandon continued sitting in the big chair. Presently a thin smiled appeared at the corners of his mouth. His conversation with Held had given him a new idea. It was true that he didn't see the need of using undue violence to achieve his ends, but if it might do so, he was quite prepared to consider it. And suddenly he saw a means both of getting rid of the nuisance posed by the old man and his sheep and dealing a blow against the Lazy Ladder. The plan would even serve a further useful purpose, keeping happy some of the wilder elements in his employ. Maybe Held was right and he had been too gentle with the old man. Maybe it was time to stop pussy-footing after all. He could eliminate the oldster and point the finger of blame at the Lazy Ladder. It wouldn't be hard to convince the marshal. He had him well under his control. And with Mitch Montgomery under suspicion of murder, it should be an easy matter to manipulate him into selling the Lazy Ladder at an even lower price than he had offered. The more he thought about it, the better he liked it. Getting to his feet, he walked to the door and went outside. The sun was blazing down and he took a few moments to admire the sweep of his property before making his way to the bunkhouse to have a further word with Held.

Between them, Utah and Seaton buried the dead sheep. It took the best part of the day following Seaton's arrival, and there were times when Seaton would willingly have abandoned the enterprise. It seemed to him then to be a waste of time and effort. The buzzards had already been at work and it would have made more sense to let them finish the job. But when he saw the anguish in the old man's eyes, he found reason to carry on. It was clear that the oldster felt a genuine affection for them, and that he blamed himself for not having done a better job of protecting them. It made no difference Seaton telling him that there was nothing he could have done. Utah felt responsible and it only made him more determined to carry on.

That evening, sitting by the campfire, they both seemed content to let the conversation turn to other matters than herding sheep.

'There's somethin' that's been puzzlin' me,' the oldster said.

'Yeah? And what's that?'

'I been kinda wonderin' where you got a name like Fark from?'

Seaton shuffled slightly and then grinned. 'It's short for Farquhar,' he replied.

'That's quite a moniker,' Utah replied noncommittally.

'What about yourself?' Seaton said, attempting to deflect the conversation and take the initiative. 'Is

28

Red your real name?'

'You know,' the oldster replied, 'I ain't rightly sure myself. But I spent a lot of time up Nevada way. Back in those days it was western Utah. Funny thing, but it was handed over by Mexico followin' the war where I got this busted leg. I guess that's where I got the name Utah. I've been around and done a lot of things since then, but it's kinda stuck.'

'How long you been herdin' sheep?'

'First time. It's a pity I didn't get into it sooner. I sure feel somethin' for those critters. Maybe it's because it's the first time anythin' has depended on me.'

Seaton stared out towards the hills and peaks, silvered by moonlight. 'Don't you get kinda lonesome?' he asked.

'I got the dogs for company as well as the sheep,' the oldster replied.

'I don't know,' Seaton mused. 'Those few days I spent in town were enough. After that, I just wanted to get away and hit the trail. But somethin' still don't feel right. Somethin' is still missin'.'

'Have you always felt that way?'

'Nope. It's just recently I guess.'

'Maybe that spell of pannin' for gold has somethin' to do with it.'

'I don't think so. I wasn't cut out to be a prospector, but it ain't that.'

'You're young. At your age, it's normal to be restless. I was that way myself once. But when I got older, I started to look at things different. Now there's nothin' much I need. I guess you could say I'm content.'

'You don't regret nothin'?'

'There's no point in regrets.' The oldster coughed and spat out some phlegm before turning back to Seaton. 'One other thing I reckon I've learned,' he said, 'and that is that the answer to some questions is nearer to home than you think.' He got to his knees and began to spread his bedroll. 'Thanks for everythin' you did today,' he said. 'I sure appreciate it.'

Seaton acknowledged his words with a wave of his arm. After the oldster had settled down, he rolled another cigarette and sat by himself, trying not to think. The sounds of the sheep had become familiar to him already so that he was barely conscious of their presence. The dogs were sleeping too, and the night was peaceful till Utah began to snore. The fire had burned low and, finishing his smoke, Seaton first checked that the chestnut was secure before turning in himself for the rest of the night.

Although he was feeling dog-tired after the day's activities, he couldn't find sleep for a long time. When it finally came it must have been deeper than usual because he didn't hear the horsemen arrive until they were almost upon the camp and had begun to open fire with their guns. In an instant he was on his feet and, seizing his rifle, he turned to face the attack. It was still dark but there was enough light for him to see three riders. The noise from their guns was deafening but even above it he heard a cry from the oldster.

'Watch out! Those sheep are on the move!'

The sheep were milling about and Red's words were barely out of his mouth before they began to run. Utah made to stand in their way and whistled to the dogs to come to him, but it was too late to take effective action. The frightened sheep were in a state of panic as the booming guns grew louder and, bleating pitiably, they started scattering in all directions.

'Leave 'em!' Seaton yelled. 'Take cover!'

He spun round and as the first riders came within range, opened fire. The effect was instantaneous. The nearest horse reared and unshipped its rider and the others came to a stop. The horse galloped clear but one of the other riders reached out a hand and hauled the fallen man up on his own mount. Seaton couldn't tell whether the man had been shot or simply unseated. He couldn't tell, either, whether any of the riders had a clear view of him or not, but it was obvious they were taken by surprise. They had imagined they had an easy target in the old man and hadn't anticipated any opposition. As he continued to fire, they began to ride away, following in the tracks of the fleeing sheep. He turned back to the oldster, who was standing behind him and looking bemused.

'Wait here!' he snapped. 'Maybe I can catch the varmints.'

He sprang to his horse and, climbing into leather, set off in pursuit. The chestnut was fast and he began to gain ground when suddenly the horse put its hoof into a gopher hole and Seaton was catapulted over its head. He landed with a thud, but the soft ground cushioned his fall. He lay there dazed, vaguely conscious of the sound of gunfire further down the valley. It went on for some time before it ceased. The sudden quiet seemed to restore him to his senses and, scrambling to his feet, he made his way to the horse, which had got back to its feet and was standing nearby.

'Are you OK, old girl?' he muttered.

A brief examination of the mare convinced him she was unhurt and he was beginning to congratulate himself on the fact that neither of them seemed to have come out of the accident too badly when the realization of what the gunfire portended suddenly broke on him. The two riders had been engaged in systematically shooting Utah's sheep.

He quickly hoisted himself back into the saddle and began to ride in the direction from which the shooting had come. He was too concerned about what he would find to care about his own safety, even when he heard further shots coming from somewhere in the distance. It didn't take him any time to find what he had dreaded. The bodies of dead and dying sheep lay all around. They had been callously massacred and not many had escaped. As he rode, the bleating of injured sheep rose into the air like a plaintive call for succour. He turned the horse and started to ride back when he saw, among the white and black corpses, first one brown object and then another. They were Utah's dogs. The first was obviously dead but when he looked more closely at the second, he noticed that its flanks were still heaving. He rode up to it and dismounted. The dog looked at him through glazed eyes and gave a faint whimper as he kneeled down beside it. He stroked it gently, observing the gaping hole where a bullet had ripped through its chest. He took its head in his hands and it made one feeble attempt to lick his hand before its eyes closed in death. Seaton got back to his feet and stood for a moment while his own eyes brimmed with tears. Then he got back into the saddle and carried on riding to where he had left the oldster.

He didn't need to tell the old man what had happened; he knew well enough for himself. Once he had ascertained that Utah was uninjured, he turned and went in search of the loose horse. He soon came up to it and, quieting it with a few whispered words, bent down to see if there was an identifying mark. It carried a brand; the horizontal interconnected lines of the Lazy Ladder. At first the name meant nothing to him. It was just a piece of information, maybe crucial information, but it was no more than that. And then the image of the girl he had spoken to back in Lindenberg flashed across his mind. What was it the older woman had said? That her father was the owner of the Lazy Ladder. He remained standing, deep in thought, before taking the horse's reins and leading it back to where Utah was sitting by the ashes of the campfire. The pinto was standing nearby.

'We'll bury these ones too,' Seaton said. 'Every last one of 'em.'

The oldster looked up at him and shook his head.

'There's no point,' he said. 'There's too many of 'em. Let the buzzards do their job.'

Seaton went over to the chestnut and fetched a flask from his saddle-bags. 'Here,' he said, handing it to the oldster. 'It might help ease things a little.'

He sat down beside him and they remained silent, passing the flask between them, while the sky gradually lightened and daylight spread across the valley. Presently Utah wiped his mouth with his sleeve.

'Those bastards,' he muttered. 'They ain't gonna get away with this. I aim to get even.'

Seaton took a swig. 'That goes without sayin',' he said.

The oldster looked at him. 'This is my problem,' he replied. 'I appreciate everythin' you've done for me, but there's nothin' else you can do now.'

'That's where you're wrong,' Seaton replied. 'The way I see it, the fact that those varmints threw lead in my direction makes it my problem too.'

Utah seemed to consider his words before replying. 'Maybe it does at that,' he said.

'What's more,' Seaton continued, 'I figure I know where to start settin' about makin' the scores even.'

Utah looked at him questioningly and Seaton nodded in the direction of the gunnie's horse.

'That hoss is carryin' a Lazy Ladder brand,' he said. He paused for a moment to let Utah reflect on his words, before asking, 'Does the name mean anything to you?'

The oldster hesitated for a moment, and then shook his head. 'I might have heard of it,' he said, 'but that's all it is – just a name.'

'You can't think of a reason why the Lazy Ladder would hold some sort of grudge against you?'

Utah shrugged. 'You said it yourself,' he replied. 'Seems like cattlemen just don't like sheep.'

'There are a number of ranches around these parts,' Seaton replied. 'They didn't all come lookin' for you.' He looked at the old man. Despite his talk of revenge, he looked bowed and Seaton was seeking for some word of hope that might help to restore something of his spirits.

'Those varmints can't have killed all those sheep,' he said. 'How many of them did you say there were?'

'Six hundred,' the oldster replied.

'Right. Let's start packin' things away here and then see if we can't find any live ones. We can round 'em up and leave 'em somewhere they'll be safe till we can get in touch with whoever is runnin' the show and get 'em to send someone else out. Unless you've still got some notion of stayin' out here yourself till September?'

The oldster didn't seem inclined to argue. It was plain he had other ideas which at least were not in conflict with Seaton's notions.

'There's only one thing I got in mind to do now,' he said. 'Whatever it takes, I'm aimin' to gain revenge for what those murderin' coyotes have done.'

When they had finished slaughtering Utah's sheep, Cooley Held and his three companions rode as hard for the Mill Iron as they could, allowing for the fact that they were one horse short. Things hadn't turned out quite as they had intended and they realized that Nash Brandon was likely to take a dim view of the way they had handled the situation, even though it hadn't really been their fault. How were they to know that the oldster wouldn't be alone? As it was, they were quite lucky to have come out of it without serious injury. However, Held was sufficiently realistic to know that Brandon wouldn't see it that way or be likely to accept any excuses. As he reflected on the matter, however, he began to feel differently. After all, they had more or less carried out their task. The sheep were either killed or scattered. Did it matter if the old man himself still survived? By the time they were approaching the ranch-house, his worries had virtually disappeared.

Once he was reassured, he signalled to the others to halt and they dismounted in order to rest the over-burdened horse with its extra rider. Keeping his words to a minimum, he outlined the situation to them. When he had finished, the man whose mount had reared and unseated him raised an objection.

'What about the horse?' he said. 'Isn't it gonna be kind of hard to explain why it's missin'?'

'What's the problem?' Held replied. 'Anythin' could have happened to it. Besides, how many horses does Brandon own? He wouldn't be able to tell you himself. He ain't likely to notice if there's one less.'

'It's the old man worries me,' one of the other two said. 'We were ordered to kill him. What if Brandon was to find out he's still alive?'

'He don't need to find out. How would he? In any case, how do we know the oldster ain't dead? We loosed a lot of lead. It's a fair bet he didn't escape gettin' cut down.'

'What's it matter anyway?' the first man said. 'What's it to Brandon whether he's dead or alive?'

The others considered his answer and after a moment the third man spoke.

'Hell,' he said, 'why are we worryin' at all? Why don't we just tell Brandon the truth? We weren't to know the oldster would have company.'

'That's what I was thinkin',' Held replied, 'but I got a feelin' it would be better not to mention the stranger. Brandon would probably expect us to have dealt with him too. No, I figure the best thing is just to say we carried out the job.'

'We didn't leave any clues like Brandon told us to.'

'So what? Anyway, we left the horse behind. That's a big enough clue, I reckon.'

The others exchanged glances. 'I reckon Held is right,' the first man said. 'The only thing we have to do is make sure no one sees the two of us ridin' in on one horse.'

'That's easily done,' Held responded. He looked at the others as they nodded in agreement. 'Fine; then that's settled. Let's get goin'.'

They remounted, the first man swinging up behind the man in the saddle, and carried on towards the Mill Iron. Held was satisfied with the outcome of their little parley, but something else which he hadn't given any thought to till now began to nag at him, and that was the identity of the stranger who had come to the oldster's assistance. He had got a decent look at him, but he didn't recognize him. Who was he? It was of no significance, but he couldn't help asking himself the question.

That night, as he lay on his bunk, the question came afresh to his mind and he found it difficult to find sleep. Despite the fact that there had been no problem with Brandon, he no longer felt as confident as he had earlier. Following from the issue of the stranger's identity, new questions began to arise. Assuming he was still alive and hadn't fallen to a stray bullet, what would the old man be likely to do next? Would he remain with the stranger? And would the stranger be likely to let the matter rest? The more he thought about it, the more certain he became that the answer to those questions wasn't likely to favour his peace of mind. He wasn't concerned that he and his fellow gunnies might have been recognized. There was little chance of that. There was no question either that the Mill Iron could be implicated. The finger of blame pointed directly to the Lazy Ladder. The horse they had left behind was branded with a Lazy Ladder emblem; stolen, just like the cattle Brandon had secreted away. There didn't seem to be too much to worry about, but all the same he felt uneasy. What if Brandon should come to learn the truth of what had happened? Was it possible he could? The oldster could turn up in Lindenberg and he could get to know about it. In fact, it was logical to expect that both the oldster and the stranger would turn up in Lindenberg. Where else would they go? The only way he would feel really safe was if they were both removed. The best chance of finding and dealing with them would be by keeping a watch on Lindenberg. The identity of the stranger was a problem, but he could be readily identified whether he showed up with or without the old man. He had a sudden thought. There was the horse. It wasn't likely the stranger would let it go; after all, it was his evidence that the Lazy Ladder was responsible. If he returned to Lindenberg, in all likelihood he would put the horse up at the livery stable. As he continued to think the matter over, his worries began to dissipate. Between them, he and his henchmen should be able to keep a close eye on events in Lindenberg. Then, once they had located the stranger and the old man, it would be easy to eliminate them. He would talk with the others tomorrow.

It took longer than either Seaton or the oldster had reckoned to round up the few sheep that remained and herd them to a sheltered part of the valley. On the following day they set off for Lindenberg. It was a slow journey since they had the extra horse in tow. Utah's whole demeanour had changed. He was quiet and withdrawn and showed little of his previous concern for the flock. They rode in silence until they approached the site of Seaton's old camp, when the oldster finally spoke.

'I've been thinkin',' he said, 'and the fact of the

matter is, I don't want to go back to Lindenberg.'

'Why not? What'll you do?'

The oldster stroked his grizzled chin. 'I was kinda thinkin' I might take up that offer you made. If it still stands, that is.'

'What offer?' Seaton replied.

'About takin' over your claim. I ain't cut out for town life. I guess I'm too used to bein' on my own.'

'I thought you said you were too old for prospectin'.'

'Maybe I am. But it's a nice spot. I reckon I could make myself comfortable here.'

Seaton didn't take much time to think about it. There wasn't much point in arguing with the oldster. If that was what he wanted, he could have it. At least he would be a lot safer than he would have been if he had remained where he was.

'OK,' he said. 'If that's what you want.'

They dismounted and he led the oldster to the stream where he had left his equipment. It was still there and he hauled it up on to the bank.

'This is my gear if you want it. I'll show you a good place to set up the tent. I'll come back with supplies when you'll be needin' 'em.'

Utah muttered his thanks and Seaton climbed back into leather. 'Sure you'll be OK?' he asked.

'Sure. You understand, don't you?'

'Yeah.' Seaton leaned down and they shook hands. 'One other thing,' he said. 'If you find any gold, it's all yours.'

He spurred the chestnut and rode away, leading

the gunman's roan. He didn't have too many concerns for the oldster this time. He was pretty sure that Utah just wanted to be alone. That was the way he chose to live. He doubted very much that Utah would even attempt to pan for gold. He knew, too, that the old timer was grieving.

When Seaton arrived in town, he had a feeling of déjà vu as he arranged for the chestnut and the roan to be placed at the livery stables and booked himself once more into the Exchange Hotel. When he had done so, he began to wander down the main street of the town, looking for the offices of the Sheepmen's Association. Utah had been more than a little vague about it, but there had to be such an organization in Lindenberg. He needed to arrange for someone to go out and tend the remnant of the sheep. There was also a little matter of Utah's wages and the absence of supplies to be dealt with. It didn't take him long to see the imposing office of the Cattle Ranch And Land Company which the barber had mentioned. He paused for a moment, wondering whether there would be any point in going inside and asking a few questions, but decided against it. He might need to do so at some point but it could wait. It might be a good idea to find out more about the Lazy Ladder first, and he intended riding over there the next day.

As he moved slowly along, his eyes couldn't help but look for Maisie Montgomery or a gig that might indicate that she was in town. He had a feeling that her connection with the Lazy Ladder was unfortunate, but he couldn't have said why. He arrived at an intersection and turned down it. It opened into a dusty square shaded by a few trees at the back of which stood a two-storey building with a number of windows, across one of which was written the words 'Marshal's Office'. It struck Seaton that the marshal would be likely to know the whereabouts of a Sheepmen's Association and made his way across to it, suddenly remembering as he did so the older lady's words accusing the marshal of not being around when he was needed. He stepped up to the door and knocked firmly. There was no response and after trying it again, he opened it and went through.

A lanky man sitting at a table drinking a cup of coffee looked up but otherwise showed little interest. Behind him, in a corner, a pot stood on an oil stove, but the aroma of coffee was fighting a losing battle with a stale, fetid smell which pervaded the room.

'Howdy,' Seaton said. 'Are you Marshal Braithwaite?'

The man looked him up and down before putting his cup down on the table. 'Who's askin'?' he said.

'The name's Seaton, but it don't signify.'

'Let me be the judge of that.'

'I can see you're a busy man, so I don't want to take up any of your time. I'm lookin' for some kind of sheepherders' association. I figured you might be the person to ask.'

At his statement the marshal's expression darkened. 'This is cattle country,' he said.

42

'Maybe so, but there's room for everybody.'

'Folk have been runnin' cattle a long time. They don't take too kindly to strangers comin' in and spoilin' the land.'

'Things change. Live and let live is what I say.'

'And not gettin' mixed up in somethin' that ain't any of your business is what I say. Who are you anyway?'

'I told you. My name's Seaton.'

'That ain't what I mean. Maybe you'd better tell me just what you're doin' in town.'

'Like I say, I got business with the sheepmen's association. If you can't help me, that's fine.'

He made a move towards the door when the marshal suddenly got to his feet and came up beside him.

'I'm keepin' my eyes on you,' he muttered. He glanced down at Seaton's gun.

'I could put you behind bars right now for carryin' an offensive weapon,' he said.

'I ain't the only one. Why don't you take time to get out and take a look around?'

'You're pushin' your luck.'

'If there's some kind of ordinance about wearin' guns, I'll obey it. If there's not – well, I guess that's just somethin' else you're gonna have to think about.'

The marshal was standing partly in his way but Seaton brushed past and went out the door. After the rank gloom of the marshal's office the daylight dazzled his eyes for a moment. He turned and began to walk down a street running parallel to the main street. Before he was out of sight he glanced back but there was no sign of Braithwaite. He hadn't succeeded in finding the place he was looking for, but he had certainly learned something about the marshal.

He carried on till he reached a run-down section of town with some weary looking stores and businesses lining the broken plank sidewalk, and was about to turn back when he noticed a low straggling building set back from the street. Although it was in a better condition than most of the other buildings, it bore the unmistakable air of being empty. What had really caught his attention, however, was the legend written across the wall: 'Lindenberg and District Sheepmen's Association'. Walking across to it, he tried the doorhandle but it was locked. He turned to the nearest window and peered inside. There was nothing unusual other than the fact that it was quite bare with just a few basic items of office furniture. A clock showed the correct time: 4.30 in the afternoon. The real thing missing was people. The place gave the impression of having been abandoned in a hurry; coffee cups stood on the tables. He stood observing the office for a few more moments, half expecting someone to appear, before turning away. On the opposite side of the street stood a carpentry shop and he made his way across.

The man inside looked up with an expression of surprise when he came through the door, as if it was an unusual event. Seaton touched his hand to his hat.

'Howdy,' he said. The man nodded. 'I was wonderin' if you could give me some information concernin' the office across the road.'

'You mean the Sheepmen's Association?' the man replied.

'Yup, that's the one. I happen to have some business with 'em and I was kinda surprised to see the place closed up.'

'You're out of luck,' the man replied. 'You should have got here a few days earlier. You've just missed 'em. Or should I say you just missed him.'

'What do you mean?'

'The sign might have said Sheepmen's Association, but I never saw more than but one man. I figured he must be kinda like the advance guard. I would have introduced myself, but I got the impression he wanted to keep himself to himself.'

'Any reason you can think of why it closed?'

The man shrugged. 'Maybe it just didn't work out. Maybe it was temporary. When I saw the man leavin' with Marshal Braithwaite, I figured it must be some sort of legal thing he was sortin' out.'

'What? The last time you saw him, he was with Marshal Braithwaite?'

'Yeah. I thought he'd be right back, but I ain't seen him since.'

'You didn't notice anythin' else unusual goin' on? About the time the place closed?'

The man thought for a moment. 'Nope,' he

replied. 'Why do you ask?'

'No particular reason, though I gather that sheep-men ain't too popular around these parts.'

The man shrugged. 'I guess not. I don't get involved. I got worries enough tryin' to keep this place goin'.' Seaton turned and made his way to the door.

'Thanks for the information,' he said.

He stepped outside and continued walking down the street away from the marshal's office, thinking over what the man in the carpenter's shop had said. His first thought was that the closure of the Sheepmen's Association seemed to coincide with the latest attack on the oldster. He was puzzled by the marshal's involvement in the affair, and was tempted for a moment to turn round and make his way back to his office, but then thought better of it. The reception he had received from Braithwaite definitely discouraged any further contact, for the present at any rate; he didn't want to take the risk of ending up behind bars. One thing was for sure; there seemed to be a lot more going on than met the eye. The only solid fact he possessed was the involvement of the Lazy Ladder in the attacks on Utah, and when he reflected on it he felt the same pang of regret that Maisie Montgomery should be incriminated in any way. There was surely no way she could personally know anything, but it jarred that there could be any suggestion of her being even faintly touched by the affair. He was feeling quite confused by his thoughts and the feelings they evoked when he turned a corner and after a few more paces emerged back on First Street.

He was at the opposite end from that which opened on to the square where the marshal had his office. Just a little way further on the street began to peter out and merge into the rolling plain that stretched to the hills, shimmering blue in the distance. He paused to look up and down the main drag. Lindenberg was a fairly nondescript little town, existing chiefly to supply the neighbouring ranches and homesteads. It was like a number of other places he had passed through and he had no desire to stay longer than he needed to. He had become embroiled in something but once it was dealt with there would be nothing to detain him. Then his thoughts once again began to stray to Maisie Montgomery and he couldn't help feeling a quickening of the pulse at the thought he might see her again the following day.

CHAPTER THREE

Utah Red had no intention of staying long at Seaton's old campsite. While it was still dark, as soon as he had eaten a meagre breakfast, he took his old Paterson rifle and filled his pocket with cartridges. From its scabbard he drew a knife and carefully ran his finger along the edge before replacing it. Then he limped over to where the skewbald was tethered, climbed on to its back and headed away from the stream towards Lindenberg. The town was not his destination, however, for when he had covered maybe a quarter of the distance he turned the horse on to a side trail which he guessed would lead him in the general direction of the Lazy Ladder. Occasionally he muttered a few words of encouragement as the pinto plodded steadily on, but otherwise his lips were drawn tight and his lined features were set in an attitude of grim concentration. He had one intention: to find the men who had killed his sheep. It didn't matter that he had only seen them briefly and in semi-darkness. He had a firm conviction that if he saw them he would recognize them. It was an

48

intuition and he trusted it.

In the scramble to escape from the intruders when they had ridden into his camp, he had caused further damage to his leg. It was hurting quite badly but he scarcely noticed it. As he rode he thought about Seaton. He had lied when he told Seaton that he hadn't heard of the Lazy Ladder. He had been around Lindenberg long enough to have learned something about most of the ranches in the area, including the Lazy Ladder. After all Seaton had done for him, he felt quite bad about it. Maybe he should have stuck with Seaton. After all, he had said himself that he was involved, that Utah's problem had become his problem too. But what did that mean? Their paths had crossed before, and he thought he knew what kind of a man Seaton was. A hard man but a good one. Maybe Seaton was out for justice, but it wasn't justice he wanted; it was revenge.

The day was getting hot and he brought the skew-bald to a halt by a trickling stream in order to let it drink. He swallowed a few mouthfuls himself from his water bottle before taking the time to examine the ground nearby, in the hope of finding any traces of the men who had killed his sheep. There were indeed indications of horsemen having ridden that way, but they could have been left by anybody. It was a long shot. No doubt there were various trails leading to and from the Lazy Ladder. Realizing the futility of what he was doing, he returned to the horse and sat down beside it. For the first time he began to consider what he would do once he arrived at the Lazy Ladder. The truth was that he just didn't know. He had set off with the sole idea of avenging his slaughtered sheep, but he hadn't given any thought as to how he was to go about it. Now, when he was well on his way, it was necessary to form some sort of plan. He couldn't just ride straight up to the ranch-house; if he did he would simply be giving his enemies the opportunity to do what they had failed to do when they attacked his camp. He had no doubts about the sort of reception he would be likely to receive. So what was the best way to go about things? He racked his brains, but he was in a quandary and thinking wasn't his forte. In the end he came to only one decision, which was that it might be sensible to wait for nightfall before arriving at the Lazy Ladder. Other than that, he gave up, trusting that something would come up. Stretching out on the grass, he lay back to rest while the sun continued its journey down the sky.

He must have dozed, because when he awoke the shadows of evening were already spreading. His head felt muggy so he went to the stream and doused it with water. Then he let the skewbald drink again before refilling his water bottle. Finally he climbed back into the saddle and continued riding as the darkness gathered and the constellations hung like bracelets in the sky. Although it was night, he could see quite clearly what lay around him. The landscape was suffused by a silvery glow and landmarks such as trees and rocks were eerily distinct, while the hills he had left behind were etched sharply against the sky.

He wasn't too sure just where he was in relation to the Lazy Ladder but he began to be more watchful while his ears were attuned to catch any sounds carried on the still night air. Once he thought he heard something, faint and far away, which vaguely suggested the snicker of a horse, but it wasn't repeated and he discounted it.

Presently his eyes discerned a few shadowy shapes, as if the darkness had thickened into something tangible; he felt suddenly nervous and it was only as he got closer that he relaxed when he saw they were the forms of cattle. Some stood singly, some lay in small groups, and he realized he must have arrived on Lazy Ladder rangeland. This was confirmed when he passed close by a dilapidated structure which he was pretty sure must have served as a line camp. He carried on riding, thinking about what he should do next, and hadn't gone very much further when he heard the faint but unmistakable sound of hoofs and then saw something move. He strained his eyes but couldn't distinguish anything. He had almost concluded that he must have been mistaken when, turning his head in a different direction, he saw the faint but unmistakable outlines of horses that were almost indistinguishable from the surrounding darkness. As quickly as his damaged leg allowed, he got down from the skewbald and drew it into the shelter of a nearby bush. He peered out but it took him a few moments to perceive the figures again. There seemed to be four riders, riding two by two with something dark in between them. For a moment he was puzzled till the group turned and he could see more clearly that the dark mass was a small group of longhorns and he understood the situation. The riders were herding the cattle and the fact they were doing so by cover of night could only mean that they were rustlers. They were probably too intent on what they were doing to notice his presence, even without the cover provided by the bush. He would have drawn his Paterson from its scabbard, but didn't want to do anything which might make the horse snicker. That was the thing he feared as he watched the scene unfold. The figures of the rustlers continued to move, at that distance appearing to do so slowly, until to Utah's relief they gradually disappeared from sight. For a while he remained where he was, listening to the fading echoes of their hoof beats in the night. When he was satisfied that they had gone and were unlikely to return, he emerged from cover, and getting on the pinto's back, rode it to where he had seen the rustlers.

He was unsure and slightly disoriented. If the Lazy Ladder was the outfit behind the attack on him and his sheep, what should his attitude be to what he had seen? He didn't like rustlers, but then it was his enemy's cattle that had been rustled. The rustlers had only done what the Lazy Ladder had done to him. On the principle that my enemy's enemy is my friend, he ought to be on their side. He was curious about who they might be and hoped he might pick up some clue to their identity, but it was a pointless task looking for clues in the dark. He was wondering

what his next move should be when he recalled the
deserted shack he had passed a little earlier. It would
do as a shelter for the night. His afternoon nap had
only served to make him more tired. In the morning
he would be in a better position to make decisions as
to how he should go about things. Turning the skewbald, he began to make his way back to the cabin.

Seaton ate a good breakfast on the morning following his encounter with the marshal and sat alone,
drinking coffee. He was conscious of a certain reluctance to be on his way to the Lazy Ladder, and he was
aware that it was because of Maisie Montgomery. It
would have been so much simpler if she wasn't
involved. She was a complication, but why should she
matter? He had only met her once. When the last
guest had left the room, he finally got to his feet and
made his way out of the hotel. Although it was early,
the sun was already bright. It was only a short walk to
the livery stables. The doors were standing open and
he passed inside, pausing a moment while his eyes
adjusted to the light. He looked around, expecting
to see the ostler, but there was no sign of him.

'Hello!' he called. 'Anybody there?'

He waited a moment before calling out again, but
there was no reply. A shaft of sunlight coming
through the door fell on the ground and he looked
down. The grimy floor bore the imprints of boots
and it was clear they had been made recently. As he
looked more closely, he saw a cigarette butt. He had
learned to trust his instincts and they were telling

him that something was not quite right.

A shadow suddenly fell across the ray of light and he turned quickly, moving aside as he did so, as shots rang out from both before and behind him. They went whistling by, missing him by inches, as he squeezed the trigger of his own gun, aiming at a shadowy figure he saw standing in the doorway. His aim was good and he heard a groan as the man reeled and then fell. He sank to one knee in order to make himself less of a target as further shots rang out from somewhere in the depths of the stable. Aiming at the flashes of flame, he fired again in reply. The horses back there were stamping and rearing and, taking advantage of the confusion, he ran forwards, zigzagging across the open space and flinging himself behind a stanchion as further shots tore into the wood and sent a shower of shards flying into the air. He was in a dark corner of the stable and couldn't see either man. The shooting had ceased and he was thinking that maybe they were trying to creep up on him when he heard someone running hard towards the runway at the back of the livery stable.

Instantly he moved away from his cover and began to follow but when he reached the open door the man had gone. At the back of the livery stable there was a corral and behind that some trees into which he had disappeared. He ran forward, risking the possibility of being fired at from the trees, but when he reached them he drew to a halt. There was no way of knowing which way the man had gone and he had a clear start. Instead, he turned and made his way back to the livery stable to see what had become of the other man. When he reached the entrance the man had gone but there was a clear trail of blood leading to an alley. He ran to it and had just turned into it when he was greeted by a couple of shots, one of which singed the material of his jacket. Realizing he was outlined against the sunlight behind him, he drew back and was considering whether to try again when away down the street he saw a group of figures coming towards him, among which he recognized the figure of the marshal. After his experience of the night before he didn't like the idea of having to face questions, so he ran quickly back to the livery stable. His chestnut mare was standing in one of the stalls and he swiftly threw a saddle across her back. He led her out the back of the livery stable and into the trees. The wooded patch extended back further than he expected but presently emerged into open country, where he stopped to adjust the saddle and fasten the girths before climbing into leather.

As he rode, he realized he had been lucky to come away with his skin intact. He had had a narrow escape, but who could his attackers be? There must be a connection with what had happened at Utah Red's camp, but what was their motive? Was it some kind of revenge attack? If that was the case, the Lazy Ladder must be involved. But then, how did they know him? During the course of the gunfight at the oldster's camp, they could have only caught a glimpse of him at best. Then the thought that they might have got the information from Utah Red himself occurred to him. If that was the case, what might they have done to the oldster? Not for the first time he felt guilty for letting Utah have his way.

Seaton was about to turn off in the direction of his old camp by the stream when he changed his mind. How would his attackers have found the old man? Of course, they might have come across him by chance, but it didn't seem likely. Another thing that puzzled him was the fact that the attack had taken place so soon after he had arrived in Lindenberg. It was as if his assailants had been waiting for him to arrive. There must have been something distinctive they were looking out for. Then the thought occurred to him; he had arrived in town leading the extra horse. That's what they had been looking out for. They must have had the town under surveillance, and especially the livery stables. Once they had spotted him, it would have been an easy matter to arrange a bushwhacking. He was probably doubly lucky in that they had not made an attempt on his life the day before. He pondered over the matter for a little longer before coming to a definite decision; he would carry on as he had intended and make his way to the Lazy Ladder. It was a pity that he had had to leave the roan behind, but it was a minor matter, even though at some point he intended recovering the cost of stabling it.

When he was sure that it was safe, Held emerged from the cover of the woods to find Marshal Braithwaite and a small group of townsmen gathered around his wounded colleague at the livery stable. The man had been shot in the arm but it wasn't serious and the town doctor was already on his way. He looked at the people gathered around, searching for the ostler, but he wasn't there and he felt pretty sure there was nothing to fear from that quarter. The ostler had seemed quite happy to receive the hefty bribe they had offered to get him out of the way and wasn't likely to put himself in the way of trouble by admitting to anything. He wasn't sure what the attitude of the marshal would be, but it was quickly apparent that he had nothing to worry about there either. Once the marshal realized the two of them were from the Mill Iron, he was immediately sympathetic.

'Looks like you boys were the victim of a premeditated attack,' he said.

'Sure seems that way. We were just passin' by when we thought we saw someone movin' about. We figured it might be horse thieves so we stopped to look inside. The next thing we knew somebody started shootin' at us.' Held turned to his companion. 'Ain't that so, Thurston?'

The other man looked up with his face contorted by pain and nodded. 'Sure, that's the way it was.'

The marshal looked round at the other people. 'OK, folks,' he said. 'Looks like we got ourselves a clear case of attempted horse theft. Guess it was lucky these folks happened by when they did. The show's over. Better get back about your business.'

They hesitated for a moment but the arrival of the

doctor at that point seemed to spur them to action and they began to move away.

'While the doc's busy here, I figure I'll just take a little look around,' the marshal said, in an attempt to look as though he was dealing with the matter. At his words a sudden thought struck Held.

'I'll give you a hand,' he said.

If he drew the marshal's attention to the horse bearing the Lazy Ladder brand, he might be able to make good the omission of clues linking the attack on the old man with the Lazy Ladder. The problem was how to link the presence of the horse with the attack on the old man. Had Brandon spoken with the marshal? He wished Brandon would keep him better informed. He couldn't see how to make the connection but at least he could point out the markings on the roan in case the marshal missed it. He was unclear as to how it might help, but maybe it would prove useful later. Making his way to the horses, he quickly found the one with the Lazy Ladder brand, the one the Mill Iron had stolen in the first place.

'Marshal!' he called. 'Over here!'

The marshal strolled across. 'What is it?' he said.

'Probably nothin',' Held replied. 'But take a look at this.' He drew attention to the markings and the marshal bent closer to investigate.

'A Lazy Ladder brand,' he said. 'So what?'

Held shrugged, attempting to look disinterested. 'I don't know,' he replied. 'What's a horse belongin' to the Lazy Ladder doin' here? They wouldn't have cause to put one of their horses up at the livery stables.'

'Maybe it's bein' shod,' the marshal replied.

'Maybe. But they got their own facilities for that kind of thing.'

The marshal looked the horse over. 'Well,' he said, 'I'll keep it in mind.'

Held had made his point and there was nothing to be gained by pursuing it further. He turned away and rejoined his comrade. The doctor had just finished removing a fragment of bullet from his forearm and bandaging up the wound.

'What do we owe you, Doc?' Held asked.

The doctor looked him up and down. 'That was a ricochet,' he said. 'Next time neither of you might be so lucky.'

Held was anxious to be away before the ostler showed up or any other awkward questions might be raised. 'Is he OK to ride?' he asked.

'Yes, but take it easy. That arm's gonna be hurtin' for a while.'

The marshal rejoined them and Held turned to him. 'OK if we go now?' he asked.

The marshal nodded. 'I know where to find you if I need you,' he said.

Held and his companion walked away into the sunlight. Their own horses were being held in the corral at the back of the stables, but Held reckoned it might be politic to return to collect them later. He could have a quick word with the ostler before they finally headed for the Mill Iron.

*

Nash Brandon came away from the latest meeting with his lawyer without having got any further with his attempt to acquire the Lazy Ladder; Mitch Montgomery still wasn't prepared to accept his latest offer. It came as no surprise to Brandon and it didn't worry him. In the days following he had other meetings both with the lawyer concerning property deals he was involved with, as well as with one or two prominent people concerning the forthcoming mayoral elections. After Held arrived back at the Mill Iron with the information that the old sheepherder had been dealt with, he was ready to put the final phase of his plan into effect. Once Montgomery was accused of the murder of the old man, he would be more than prepared to sell the Lazy Ladder for a fraction of its real value – especially if Brandon were to offer the services of his lawyer in Montgomery's defence. Brimming with confidence, he strutted down the main street of Lindenberg feeling generally satisfied with the way things were going.

His first appointment at the bank was quickly dealt with, and he was about to direct his footsteps to the marshal's office when he was just in time to see Maisie Montgomery enter the Broadway Coffee Shop. The sight of her caused him to change his mind and he began to make his way to there. He strode briskly and entered the establishment only moments after her, but he was disappointed to see that she was not alone but was sitting opposite another woman whom she had obviously arranged to meet. He felt a pinch of disappointment and annoyance and would have gone back out again except for fearing some loss of face. Instead, he made his way to another table at the back of the room, bowing slightly and raising his hat as he passed them both. The waitress came over and took their order before approaching him.

'Coffee,' he said curtly.

His eyes briefly followed her as she walked away before he fell to surreptitiously observing Maisie and her companion. Though the charms of the other woman were undeniable, the comparison worked all in Maisie's favour and only served to quicken his desire for her. They were talking quite animatedly, but though he strained his ears to try and catch something of what they were saying he could only pick out odd disconnected words and phrases. When she mentioned the name of her father his interest was even further aroused and he leaned forward across the table. From what he could make out, it seemed she was saying something about Montgomery not being his usual self of late. The name of Mowbray, the town doctor, was mentioned. He had to piece together what she was saying and maybe he was getting it all wrong, but it seemed that Mitch Montgomery was feeling the pressure. He wondered just how much Maisie knew. Was she aware that he had made an offer for the Lazy Ladder? Somehow he had a feeling that the situation might offer scope for putting pressure on Maisie Montgomery to accede to his advances. It was certainly something worth thinking about. The conversation between Maisie and her companion seeming to have moved on to other things, he got to his feet and made his way to the counter, courteously lifting his hat once again as he passed their table. When he had left the coffee shop, he paused for just a moment to take a look up and down Front Street before turning on his heels and making his way to the marshal's office.

Braithwaite was looking out of the window when he saw Brandon's advancing figure. Immediately he did so he moved quickly to his desk, capped the bottle of whiskey which stood there and put it in a drawer along with the tumbler from which he had been drinking. He replaced them with some papers and had just started to riffle through them when the door opened and the rancher entered.

'Mr Brandon,' he said. 'It's sure good to see you.'

Without replying, Brandon took a chair and produced a large cigar from an inside pocket, which he proceeded to cut and trim before lighting it and placing it in his mouth. He drew in a mouthful of smoke and then turned to the lawman.

'I won't beat about the bush,' he said. 'I have reason to believe that a serious crime has been committed and I want you to go and investigate.'

'Why of course, Mr Brandon. May I ask what kind of offence?'

'My suspicions are that it may be murder: cold-blooded murder. Not only that, but the murder of a poor defenceless old man.'

The marshal was taken aback and his features

showed his state of confusion.

'As you know, there have been moves afoot of late to introduce sheep into the area,' Brandon continued. 'It's common knowledge that the Sheepmen's Association took on someone to look after a flock up in the hills. I fear for that man's safety.'

'Why? I mean, what reason. . . .'

'I have my ear to the ground. In my position it pays to know what is going on. I can't say more than that, much less begin to think of pointing the finger of blame. As a good citizen, I simply bring the matter before you.' Brandon inhaled deeply and then rose to his feet.

'I must be off,' he said. 'I have every confidence that you will handle this matter in the appropriate way. In fact, I could let you have one of my men. I'm sure I could spare somebody who knows his way about those hills.' He strode to the door and paused before turning the handle.

'You have made a good job of being marshal,' he said. 'If I am fortunate enough to be voted mayor, I shall certainly bear that in mind.'

He turned and went out. The marshal sat back in his chair and after a few moments got out the bottle of whiskey and refreshed his glass. He swallowed it down and then poured another, thinking as he did so about what Brandon had said. He wasn't entirely sure how to take it, but he knew enough to realize where his best interests lay.

Marshal Braithwaite could put two and two together and get them to make four. It was obvious that Brandon wished to incriminate someone, and he had given a broad hint that it was to be one of the ranchers. He knew that Brandon had his eyes on the Lazy Ladder, and then coincidentally the Lazy Ladder was implicated in the shootout at the livery stable. It was a fair guess that if he rode up into the hills he would find the body of the old man together with something that could be used as evidence against the Lazy Ladder. To have to do so was a nuisance, but he could see no way of avoiding it. It might seem a circuitous route for Brandon to achieve his ends, but that was how he went about things. Brandon wasn't given to plain speaking. He was a man on the up and it was important to him not to give anything away which might later be held against him. He had political ambitions; that was enough to enjoin caution. So it was with an ill humour that he awaited the arrival of Brandon's man, and when he duly turned up, rode out of Lindenberg on his spurious quest. He knew what role he had to play and what the outcome would be. He realized the pointlessness of the whole exercise, but he needed to act out the part that Brandon had assigned him.

It didn't take Marshal Braithwaite long to locate Utah Red's old camp. After all, he had Brandon's man to help him, and that particular individual made small effort to conceal the fact that he knew perfectly well where it was. It was when they got there that things seemed to go somewhat awry, because neither of them could find the old man's body nor evidence pointing to anyone's involvement in some kind of nefarious activity. All they had to go on were some stray corpses of sheep and it would have been difficult to tell from their condition that they had even been shot. It was plain to the marshal that his companion was completely nonplussed by the turn of events. He had clearly been expecting to find evidence that could be used to incriminate somebody who might get in Brandon's way and the marshal had a shrewd idea that it was Mitch Montgomery and the Lazy Ladder. He'd had enough anyway of the whole charade.

'It's pretty clear to me,' he said, 'that somethin' ain't right.'

'What do you mean?' the man from the Mill Iron replied.

'Isn't it obvious? Those sheep. Somethin' killed 'em. So what happened to whoever was lookin' after 'em? And where's the rest of the flock?'

'Yeah, of course.'

'And what's more,' Braithwaite continued, 'I got my suspicions about who's responsible.'

'Oh yeah?' the man replied dubiously.

'I can't say anythin' more, but let's just say I intend payin' a visit to the Lazy Ladder.'

It was a calculated shot and the response it evoked convinced the marshal that he was right about the Lazy Ladder being Brandon's intended target. His companion's attitude of puzzlement and despondency immediately changed to one of eagerness.

'I bet you're right,' he said.

'If we had more men and more time I figure we'd

turn up some evidence, but it doesn't make any difference. I intend gettin' to the bottom of this and if the Lazy Ladder is responsible for any wrongdoing, I'll see to it that they pay.'

'You're the one to bring 'em to justice.'

'OK,' Braithwaite said, 'I reckon we've done all we can up here. Let's get back now so I can carry on my investigations and you can report back to Mr Brandon.'

The man from the Mill Iron showed some reluctance to leave without having anything more concrete to show for his trip, but the marshal's words did their trick. After a final glance over Utah's old camp, they climbed into leather and began the ride back to Lindenberg.

As Seaton rode towards the Lazy Ladder, he tried to put everything from his mind apart from what he intended to say to Mitch Montgomery. If Montgomery was the sort of person who would attack an old man, what kind of a hearing could he expect? As he got closer, he paid greater attention to his surroundings, half expecting to be met by an unwelcome reception committee comprised of Montgomery's most hardened cowpokes. As he looked about for any signs of potential hostility, he thought about his meeting with Maisie Montgomery and couldn't help noticing the irony of the fact that the roughnecks who had burst into town on that occasion, threatening life and limb with their casual shooting, were cowboys from the Mill Iron, not the

Lazy Ladder.

He knew he was on the Lazy Ladder range when he began to see cattle. They were scattered about, grazing, and they looked in prime condition. He brought the chestnut to a halt in order to appreciate the scene. There was an atmosphere of peace about it, which did not chime in either with notions of the Lazy Ladder being responsible for violence directed towards the oldster and his sheep or Seaton's own tangle of emotions. The place seemed to be aptly named. He rode on and presently came in view of the ranch-house. It was a compact, two-storey building with a raised veranda, at the back of which were several smaller buildings and a couple of corrals. On one side stood a grove of trees and on the other a small garden had been laid out. It looked neat and homely. What caught Seaton's attention in particular was a buggy standing in a corner of the yard which he recognized as the one Maisie Montgomery had been driving on the day of their encounter. Did it signify she was at home? He felt a slight quiver of anticipation as he moved forward and rode into the yard of packed earth, where he dismounted and tied his horse to the hitching rail. At close quarters the ranch-house looked even more snug and inviting. There were gathered curtains at the windows, with ornaments and vases of flowers on the window ledges and window boxes and pots with plants in them outside. Seaton fancied he saw the hand of Maisie Montgomery in all this and, thinking of her, it was with some trepidation that he stepped up on to the veranda and knocked on the ranch-house door.

He wasn't prepared when, after a few moments, the door was opened by Miss Maisie herself. He was taken aback and thrown into a state of confusion, but if Miss Maisie was at all disconcerted, she did not show it.

'Why,' she said, 'this is an unexpected surprise. It's Mr Seaton, isn't it? Won't you come on in?'

He entered the room, removing his Stetson, and stood a little awkwardly.

'Won't you take a seat?' she said, indicating a stiff-backed chair. He sat down and she sat opposite him.

'How are you finding things in Lindenberg?' she asked. 'I am assuming you are fairly new to the area.'

'It's a nice town,' he replied.

'It is most of the time,' she responded. There was a moment's silence before she continued, 'You must excuse me. I'm not being a very good hostess. Can I get you some refreshment? Coffee perhaps?'

Seaton, sitting upright with his hat on his knees, realized that some explanation of his presence was required.

'Miss Montgomery,' he began. 'It's me who should be askin' to be excused. I wouldn't have intruded on you like this but... the thing is, I need to have a word with your father.'

'Need,' she repeated. 'That sounds quite serious.'

Seaton was struggling to reply, but she saved him the effort by getting to her feet.

'Coffee,' she said. 'I think we might both use a cup.'

She walked across the room and through a door leading to what Seaton guessed was the kitchen. While she was gone he tried to think of the best way to explain to her what he was doing there, beginning to wish he hadn't come while at the same time feeling there was nowhere else he would rather be. After a few minutes she reappeared carrying a tray on which stood a pot of coffee and two matching porcelain cups and a jar. She placed the tray on a table and proceeded to pour.

'Milk?' she asked.

'No thank you. I'll take it black.'

She handed him the cup and sat down before taking up her own. 'I don't know your first name,' she said.

It was a remark Seaton hadn't been expecting. 'It's Fark,' he replied. He expected her to show some reaction, but if the name sounded strange to her she didn't show it. She smiled and lifting the coffee to her lips, took a sip before speaking.

'May I ask you something? Your visit here; has it anything to do with the Mill Iron?'

Seaton returned her glance and their eyes held each other for just a moment longer than was necessary.

'No, it hasn't,' he replied. 'But might I ask you the reason you thought it might be?'

'Oh,' she said, dropping her eyes, 'I shouldn't really have said anything. It's really none of my business. But I've been very concerned about my father recently. Normally he's very relaxed and easy going, but just lately he's changed. He's become tense and withdrawn and I'm sure it has something to do with the Mill Iron. He likes to keep the running of the ranch his private concern, but I'm sure the owner of the Mill Iron wants to extend his property by buying the Lazy Ladder.'

'Is the owner of the Mill Iron a man by the name of Brandon?'

She glanced at him again. 'How did you know that?' she asked.

'I heard some talk. From what I gather, he's quite a big noise in the county.'

A faint look of distaste touched her fine features. 'Yes,' she replied. 'In a way I suppose the town owes him quite a lot, but I don't like him. My father would never sell the Lazy Ladder, but I can see that he's worried.' Suddenly her poise seemed to waver. 'I'm sorry,' she said. 'I shouldn't be talking to you like this. After all, you're almost a stranger.'

'I appreciate your confidence and you can rest assured that I have no connection with the Mill Iron. I came to see your father on a different matter entirely. There was an incident in which a friend of mine, an old sheepherder, was attacked by some men. I am just trying to find out who they were.'

The look of concern on her face was suddenly replaced by one of indignation.

'My father would never be involved in anything of that nature,' she exclaimed, 'and neither would any of his employees. I think you must have come to the wrong place.'

'I'm sorry,' Seaton said, 'I didn't mean to imply anything. My only starting point is that it's well known that cattle ranchers and sheepmen don't tend to see eye to eye.'

'If any cattle ranchers, as you put it, are responsible for the attack on your friend, it wouldn't be my father,' she said.

'I'm sure of that,' he replied.

She took another sip of coffee and when she looked at him again, she seemed to have resumed her previous attitude.

'You must feel some affection for this old man,' she said, 'if you're prepared to take up his cause. I do hope he wasn't injured.'

'Nope, at least not seriously, but most of his sheep were killed.'

Seaton finished his cup of coffee. He felt that the time had come for him to make his departure but at the same time was reluctant to do so. Placing his cup on the table, he rose to his feet.

'It's been very nice talking to you, Miss Montgomery,' he said, 'but I mustn't impose on you further.'

She uttered a little rippling laugh.

'Of course you're not imposing,' she said. 'Why not stay and have another cup of coffee? My father should be back before long. It would be a pity for you to come all this way and not see him.'

'That's OK,' Seaton replied, 'maybe another time.'

'I hope so,' she replied. She got to her feet and they walked together to the door where he stood for a moment before putting on his Stetson.

'I'll tell him you called,' she said.

He went outside, and untying his horse, swung into the saddle.

'Thank you for all the hospitality,' he said.

Touching his hand to the brim of his hat, he swung the horse round and headed out of the yard. When he looked back, she was still standing on the veranda watching him. She lifted her hand and waved and he waved to her in return. Then he settled in the saddle and rode away. His mind was racing and he was torn by a conflict of emotions. In a sense he had achieved nothing by coming to the Lazy Ladder, or at least nothing firm and concrete. But of one thing, intuitively, he was sure. The Lazy Ladder was innocent of the attack on Utah.

CHAPTER FOUR

The line cabin in which Utah Red had taken shelter for the night was little better than a dugout, but as far as he was concerned it was positively luxurious. He was used to spending his nights in a flimsy tent or out in the open, and to sleep on a mattress, however dirty and worn, was a rare treat. Recent events had worn him down so it was no surprise that when he woke, the sun was already high. Although he had slept well, his head felt heavy and he flinched away from the light that poured down on him through a cracked windowpane. Dragging himself upright, he stumbled outside to relieve himself and then returned inside to make something to eat. In one corner of the cabin stood a small wood-burning stove propped up with a stack of flat rocks where one leg was missing, and a few logs. Lifting the lid, he scraped about among some cold grey ashes before putting in some kindling and wood and lighting a fire. He put a pot of water on the back and threw in a few coffee grounds before rummaging through his meagre supplies, which he had brought in with him the previous night, and placing a slab of sowbelly in a battered frying pan. While it was cooking he went back out and grained the skewbald.

While he was eating, he thought about what his next move should be but still couldn't arrive at a definite plan. He was beginning to regret his decision to part with Seaton. What was he doing now? He had said he would return at some point with fresh supplies. How would Seaton react when he found he was gone? Finishing his meal, he got to his feet and walked to the door. Suddenly he tensed. A rider was approaching. He was still some way off, but he was definitely heading for the line cabin. He cursed under his breath for having lighted the stove. It was probably the smoke that had attracted the man's attention. He turned back inside the cabin and began to gather his things together but quickly realized there was no way he would be able to get away before the man arrived. All he could do would be to pretend he had lost his way and sought shelter for the night. It was almost the truth. Normally, his presence there wouldn't have presented any problems, but he had more than enough experience of the Lazy Ladder's methods to fear the worst. No, his only chance was to take the offensive. Quickly, he grabbed his Patcrson where it stood against the wall, and took up a position next to the window.

The rider came slowly on. Utah's eyes weren't as sharp as they once were, and he screwed them up in the effort to see more clearly. As the man got closer, it seemed to him that there was something vaguely familiar about him and his pulses quickened. Could he be one of the men who had attacked him and killed his sheep? One of the men he was looking for? If so, he would have no regrets about shooting him. Who else could it be? But he had only had a brief sight of the men concerned; he couldn't be sure, not sufficiently sure to pull the trigger unless he really had to. But if he waited till the man revealed his identity, it would be too late. He licked his lips and his finger tightened on the trigger.

When he was still some distance away, the man brought his horse to a halt and, cupping his mouth with his hand, shouted, 'Utah Red! Is that you in there?'

The oldster didn't reply. He was puzzled. How did the man know his name? Was it some kind of trick? The man repeated his call, and when there was no response, carried on riding. He wasn't being careful in any way and showed no hint of apprehension. He certainly wasn't taking any precautions against a hostile reception – quite the opposite. He came steadily on, riding at the same pace, but it was only when he had almost reached the line cabin that the oldster recognized him.

'Me oh my!' he muttered to himself. 'If it ain't Fark Seaton!'

Laying the gun aside, he moved to the door and stepped outside. Seaton's reaction on seeing him was one of surprise.

'Utah!' he exclaimed. 'What in tarnation are you

doin' here? I thought I'd left you at the diggin's! I thought I recognized that old skewbald.' He slid from the saddle and, coming together, they embraced.

'I could ask you the same question,' Utah said.

Seaton took a glance at the cabin. 'Is that coffee I can smell?' he said.

The oldster grinned. 'Sure is. I just finished a pot, but it won't take but a few minutes to brew up a fresh one.'

Seaton fastened the chestnut and they went inside. 'Nice place you got here,' he said.

He flung himself into a broke-back chair while the oldster did the honours. In no time at all they were drinking strong black coffee and enjoying the acrid taste of Seaton's tobacco.

'OK,' Seaton said. 'You go first. I figure you've got some explainin' to do.'

Utah gave a brief account of his activities, and when he reached the part about the rustlers, he really caught Seaton's attention.

'You're sure about what you saw?' he asked.

'Yeah, of course. I've been around long enough to know when somethin's afoot.'

'You figure you can find the spot?'

'Sure. It ain't any distance. But I shouldn't think you'll find anythin'.'

'Maybe not,' Seaton replied, 'but we should be able to pick out the rustler's sign.'

Utah looked at him questioningly. 'Before we do that,' he said, 'I figure you've got some explainin' to do too.'

Seaton's account was brief and to the point. It wasn't only that he didn't want to get bogged down in details, but he didn't know what to make of it all himself. When he had finished the oldster shook his head.

'I don't understand it,' he said. 'You say the Sheepmen's Association building was empty? I guess that's why I never received any supplies. So what could have happened to Brown?'

'Brown?' Seaton asked.

'Brown is the man who gave me the job.'

Seaton's interest was aroused. 'What did this man Brown look like?'

The oldster shrugged. 'I don't know,' he replied, 'it's hard to say.'

'Was he young? Was he old? There must be somethin'.'

'He was about your age, I reckon. I can't remember anythin' much about him. He was kinda average, I guess.'

Seaton gave the oldster an exasperated look. 'Well,' he said, 'I guess it doesn't much matter. He's probably far away by now. Still, if there was a chance of him still bein' around, it might be interestin' to hear what he has to say.'

'I guess so, but nothin' you've said means that the Lazy Ladder couldn't be involved in all this.'

'I just don't see it,' Seaton replied.

'OK, but if it wasn't the Lazy Ladder, then who is responsible?'

'That's why it would be interestin' to hear what your man Brown has to say. By the way, isn't it kind of a coincidence that he's called Brown and you can't seem to recall much about him?'

'How do you mean?'

'He seems to be pretty anonymous all round. What's the bettin' that Brown isn't his real name? Maybe I'm talkin' nonsense, but it could be he knew he was puttin' himself in the way of danger tryin' to introduce sheep into the area. But leavin' that aside, just think about somethin' else for a moment. What other name seems to be croppin' up?'

'I don't know. You tell me.'

'Brandon. He seems to be the big man round these parts, but I get the impression folks don't like him. Now he wants to acquire the Lazy Ladder, the very ranch that seems to be involved with tryin' to drive you out. Don't you think that's somethin' of a coincidence?'

The oldster still looked puzzled. 'They were doin' more than tryin' to drive me out,' he replied. 'If you hadn't have come along when you did, I figure I'd be dead by now.'

Seaton was thoughtful. 'What do you reckon?' he asked. 'Somebody who'd rustle cattle wouldn't be likely to draw the line at stealin' horses.'

A dawning light glimmered in the oldster's eyes. 'That horse they left behind,' he said. 'It carried a Lazy Ladder brand.'

'That's right, but that doesn't mean the Lazy Ladder was involved. What if those cattle rustlers are horse thieves too?'

The oldster nodded his head slowly. 'Yeah. I think I see what you're drivin' at. Then that would mean. . . .'

'Exactly. Whoever was responsible for the horse thievin' and the cattle rustlin' would be behind it all.'

'It doesn't necessarily follow.'

'No, it doesn't, but it's a good bet.'

Seaton swallowed the last of the coffee and got to his feet. 'Come on,' he said, 'let's you and me take a look at where you figure you saw the rustlin' goin' on. Those varmints must have left tracks. We don't need to speculate about who might be responsible. If we can follow their trail, we should have some answers.'

A short time later they set off, Seaton riding the chestnut and Utah his pinto. As they rode slowly along, Seaton kept his eyes on the ground, searching for any sign the rustlers would have left. It was likely that they had covered a decent amount of ground and he didn't want to rely on the oldster's sense of direction. It was night when he had observed the rustlers, and it would be no fault of his if he were a little imprecise in his calculations. He had misjudged the oldster, however, because they hadn't gone too far when they found what they were looking for. In order to maximise their chances of finding something, they had split up and were riding at a little distance from each other when Utah began to shout.

'Over here! I think I've found somethin'!'

Seaton rode over. Utah had got down from the

skewbald and was examining the ground. It didn't take much skill in the art of tracking, however, to realize that riders had passed that way. The ground was churned up by hoofs and it was apparent that it wasn't only horses that had made them.

'Some of those marks were made by cow critters,' Utah said, 'and they were on the run.'

Seaton felt a surge of excitement run through him. 'You figure you can follow the trail?' he asked. 'I ain't so good at trackin'.'

'I reckon so,' the oldster replied. 'Leastways, for the time bein'.'

'OK. Looks like we're on to somethin'. Let's get goin'.'

Utah pulled a wry face. 'How do you know they weren't made by some of the Lazy Ladder boys?' he asked.

'I don't know, but they're right here where you figure you saw those riders last night and it looks like whoever made 'em was runnin' down cattle. It doesn't look to me like they were left by any Lazy Ladder cowpokes.'

The oldster grunted in assent and they remounted. Following the sign was quite easy; apart from the prints left on the grass, there was plenty of evidence in the form of droppings.

'My hunch is that the trail will lead us right to the Mill Iron if we can follow it to the end,' Seaton remarked. 'Have you any idea in which direction it is?'

The oldster shook his head. 'I ain't altogether

sure, but from what I've heard, I figure this way is probably about right.'

As they rode, they saw cattle, but gradually their numbers began to thin. The terrain became more broken with clumps of thickets and underbrush.

'Brush bustin' country,' Utah remarked.

'Yeah. I've worked this type of terrain in my time, and it ain't easy.'

It became more difficult to follow the trail and from time to time they had to stop and dismount to take a closer look at the sign. There were times when Seaton found it hard to discern anything at all, but the oldster proved his mettle.

'I done some scoutin' once,' he said. 'A long time ago. I guess you don't forget these things.'

'Who was that for?' Seaton asked. 'Old Hickory?'

The oldster grinned but didn't elucidate. They carried on riding, going slowly, matching the chestnut's pace to that of the pinto. The sun sank low in the sky and the shadows of evening were gathering when Seaton rode close to the oldster.

'It's gettin' too hard to make things out. We'd better think about settin' up camp,' he said.

'Suits me,' Utah replied. 'I reckon the horses would appreciate a rest too.'

They rode a little further till they saw a suitable spot where a rivulet rippled by in the shade of some bushes.

'We must have left the Lazy Ladder behind,' Utah said.

'Yeah. A while ago I reckon.'

To the right of them the land rose gradually to meet a low line of hills in the distance.

'My sheep are up there,' the oldster mused.

'They'll be OK.'

Seaton wasn't sure whether they would be or not. He had intended to arrange for someone to go up there to mind them, but since the Sheepmen's Association headquarters was closed down, he hadn't been able to. He remembered the sound of the wolf howling the night he had spent there with the oldster. Whether Utah was thinking similar thoughts he couldn't tell. Since the shooting he seemed to have lost some of his interest in the sheep. It was as though something inside him had been lost when they died. Had it been replaced by his desire for revenge?

When Held and his injured companion collected their horses later in the day of the shootout with Seaton, they had already elaborated a story that would account for the man's injury without getting involved in the actual facts of the case. That could cause complications. They were both hoping that they might avoid having to explain at all so it was with some trepidation that, some time later, they saw Brandon himself approach as they were working on some drainage.

'Held!' he cried. 'I've been lookin' for you.' He looked at the wounded man's bandaged arm. 'Hello,' he continued, 'what happened here?' Held and his companion quickly exchanged glances.

'It's like this,' Held began. 'We were workin' down the boundary line, repairin' fences, when we spotted a rider comin' towards us. We didn't think anything of it but when he saw us he started to hightail it. It looked kinda suspicious so we got to our horses and rode after him. He opened fire and Thurston here took one in the arm. We carried on ridin' but he had too big a start on us and he got away.'

Brandon nodded. 'You can't blame yourselves for that,' he said. He took a close look at the injured man's arm.

'Someone did a good job of bandaging it,' he said, turning to Held. 'Was that you?'

Held nodded. 'I always carry some medical supplies,' he mumbled. 'You never know when they might be needed.'

'Indeed not. You managed to remove any traces of lead?'

'Yeah.'

'That's a mighty handy skill to have,' Brandon replied. Held nodded.

'This stranger,' Brandon resumed after a few moments, 'the one that shot Thurston; he wouldn't by any chance be the one you had some trouble with at the livery stable recently?'

Held turned but avoided facing Brandon directly. 'Trouble at the livery stable,' he repeated. 'I'm not sure. . . .'

'Don't lie to me,' Brandon hissed. The expression on his face had changed from one of mild affability to a scowl of anger. 'Marshal Braithwaite was over this afternoon. I know the whole story. I know something else as well.' He paused but there was no response from either man.

'Don't you want to know what it is?'

Held licked his lips and Thurston merely nodded.

'This isn't the only lie you've told me. Braithwaite took a ride into the hills recently in order to investigate a little matter of the murder of an old sheepherder. He was expecting to find some evidence but he told me that despite taking a good hard look, he couldn't find anything. Now isn't that strange seein' as how you boys were specially commissioned to provide it?'

Held was trying desperately to think of some excuse, but he knew he was beaten.

'There's somethin' else as well,' Brandon continued, addressing Held in particular. 'It seems like you were particularly keen to draw his attention to the brand markings on a horse right there in the livery stable. It was the Lazy Ladder. Now I wonder what that was doin' there?'

Held and the other man were both silent as Brandon looked hard first at one and then the other. His face was drawn tight in a rictus of rage. He seemed to be struggling to remain in control of himself, but with an effort he succeeded.

'I think you've got some explaining to do,' he said. 'I don't know where Rogan is, but you'd better find him quick. I want to see all three of you in my study in an hour.'

Without waiting for a reply, he turned and rode

away. Held and Thurston remained where they stood, as if transfixed by Brandon's malice, until Held spoke again.

'Better do as he says,' he muttered.

'What do you think is goin' to happen?' Thurston replied.

'I don't know, but we'll be lucky to come out of it in one piece. We'd better be quick and find Rogan.'

With sinking hearts, they went to their horses and climbed into leather.

Seaton and Utah broke camp early in the morning and after making a decent breakfast, set off once more. The oldster reckoned he could just about make out the trail the rustlers had left but it got progressively harder to find it. After riding for some little distance further, they had to admit defeat.

'What do we do now?' Utah asked.

'There's nothin' else we can do except keep ridin' in the same direction.'

The character of the country had changed again and had become grassier. Presently, towards noon, they caught a glimpse of some kind of structure ahead of them.

'What is it?' Utah said.

'I don't know. Pity I had to leave my field glasses behind.'

When they had ridden a little further they could hear a faint creaking noise and the nature of the object was revealed; it was a windmill and it was standing a little back from a wire fence.

'I ain't seen one of those danged things around here,' Utah remarked.

'Me neither, but together with that fence, I guess it probably means we've reached Mill Iron range.'

They sat their horses and regarded the unfamiliar scene. The windmill was a crude wooden affair with a big wooden wheel and double vanes. A ladder ran up one side.

'Looks like we ain't gonna get any further,' Utah said.

They rode up to the fence. It was well set and braced with posts at regular intervals and four strands of wire.

'Guess it's goodbye to the open range, at least as far as Brandon is concerned,' Seaton said.

'If this is the Mill Iron and we're right about those rustler varmints, there must be a way in someplace.'

'Yeah, but not just here. I guess we left their trail somewhere.'

They turned their mounts and rode parallel to the fence for a little way.

'Brandon must be doin' real well,' Seaton said. 'All this must cost a lot of money.'

They drew to a halt. 'So what do we do now?' Utah said.

'We've done what we set out to do,' Seaton replied. 'I think we can be pretty sure those rustlers came from the Mill Iron. If so, it's a pretty safe bet it's not the first time. So what does that say about Brandon and his methods? I'd say that if any cattle outfit was responsible for the attack on you, it's more likely to be the Mill Iron than the Lazy Ladder.'

'There ain't no proof,' Utah replied.

Seaton glanced along the line of the fence. 'It must have taken some time to set this up,' he said, 'and a lot of labour. I wonder how many men Brandon employs?'

'You figure it'll catch on?' Utah asked.

'I guess so,' Seaton said. As he glanced along the line of the fence another thought occurred to him. 'Remember me telling you about my visit to the Lazy Ladder?' The oldster nodded.

'Miss Montgomery said she thought Brandon had made an offer for it to her father. Well, it seems to me that if a man wanted to make life difficult for a neighbour, one way would be to fence him in.'

There was a brief silence before Utah spoke. 'What are you gonna do? Head back for Lindenberg?'

Seaton looked at him. 'What am I gonna do? Don't you mean what are we gonna do?'

The oldster grinned awkwardly. 'Yeah, that's what I meant,' he said.

Seaton thought for a moment. 'I figure I could have a problem there. After what's happened, the marshal is likely to be lookin' out for me.'

'Are you sure he'd recognize you?'

'No I'm not, but it's a big risk.' He scratched his head.

'If you need someplace to hide out, there's always the line cabin.'

Seaton shook his head. 'We ain't got a right to stay

there,' he said. 'Besides, it would be only a question of time before somebody showed up.'

He remained deep in thought, trying to puzzle out what the next move should be, when his face brightened.

'I've got it,' he said. 'We will head back to Lindenberg after all, and when we get there we'll make ourselves at home in the old Sheepmen's Association building. It's standin' empty and there's no reason the marshal would know we were makin' use of it. If he's lookin' out for me at all, he'll be keepin' his eyes on the hotel.'

'Sounds as good a plan as any,' Utah replied.

'It'll do for the time bein',' Seaton said.

When Held and his two companions entered the ranch-house, they were immediately taken aback by seeing Marshal Braithwaite sitting in a chair next to Brandon. They hesitated for a moment in the doorway.

'Come on in,' Brandon said. 'I think you already know Marshal Braithwaite?' Held mumbled something in reply.

'I told you the marshal was over earlier. I forgot to mention I invited him to stay on for a while.'

Some chairs had been drawn up for them to sit in and after they had done so Brandon briefly made the introductions. He and the marshal both held glasses in their hands and there was a bottle of brandy on a table, but Brandon pointedly did not offer them any. When he had completed the formalities, Brandon turned to his foreman.

'I won't beat about the bush,' he said. 'In view of what has occurred, I ought to sack all three of you. You lied to me and you let me down badly. However, I might be prepared to make excuses, subject to certain conditions.'

Although Brandon's manner was firm and unyielding, Held thought he detected a slight change from the outright anger and hostility he had shown earlier. He wasn't sure whether to put it down to the drink or some other factor.

'Whatever you say, Mr Brandon,' he replied, acting as spokesman for the group. 'We realize we did the wrong thing and we're real sorry.'

Brandon, apparently ignoring his words, carried on with his theme. 'Marshal Braithwaite has informed me of events at the livery stable. It seems that the man with whom you got in a tangle is already known to him.'

'Sure is,' Braithwaite intervened. 'He came into my office the day before askin' questions about the Sheepmen's Association. I made some enquiries at the Exchange Hotel. Seems like his name is Seaton.'

'Apparently this same man Seaton is responsible for the disappearance of an old timer the Sheepmen's Association took on to look after a flock in the hills near town,' Brandon continued. 'In view of what you and the marshal have said concerning a horse which apparently belonged to him, he may also be in the employ of the Lazy Ladder ranch. The evidence is conclusive. I have discussed what should now be done with the marshal, and we are agreed that Seaton must be found and brought to justice.'

He paused to take a drink. Held thought he knew which way the conversation was heading, but he couldn't be entirely sure.

'Like Mr Brandon says,' Braithwaite added, taking up the theme, 'this man Seaton is dangerous and needs to be dealt with. To that end Mr Brandon has been kind enough to let me have the use of your services.'

'If you are agreeable,' Brandon resumed, 'you will act, as it were, as unofficial deputies and your role is to bring this man in dead or alive.' He glanced at the wounded man. 'You can stay behind,' he said.

It seemed to Held that the emphasis of his final statement fell on the word 'dead' as Brandon looked squarely at him.

'Of course, Mr Brandon,' he replied. 'We'll be more than happy to work with the marshal and do whatever it takes. We appreciate the opportunity to make amends for all our previous mistakes and this time we certainly won't let you down.'

Brandon grinned. 'You'd better not,' he replied. He turned to Braithwaite. 'Well, Marshal,' he said, 'there you have it. My men are more than willing to work with you in the interests of upholding law and order and keeping the town safe. And if I may say so, I think that is an excellent outcome to our little discussion.'

He raised his glass and the marshal did likewise; they both took another draught before Brandon turned back to Held.

'You boys can go now. Until further notice, you're workin' with the marshal.'

The interview was over and Held and his two associates made their way outside. When the door had closed behind them Brandon leaned towards the marshal and replenished their glasses.

'Whoever this man is,' he said, 'I want him killed. As far as the Lazy Ladder is concerned, you can leave that to me.'

'Mitch Montgomery still holding out?' the marshal asked.

'He's proving stubborn but I think a little fire might help to persuade him.'

The marshal laughed. 'A fire?' he asked.

'It's been a dry season,' Brandon replied. 'If the wind gets up, anything could happen.'

Braithwaite glanced out of the window with an assumed look of concern on his face.

'Seems to be gettin' up a breeze right now,' he joked. They both laughed.

'If Montgomery loses his winter feed, he'll have to sell off his cattle at a loss.'

The marshal guffawed again. 'The ones he's still got left,' he replied.

Brandon shot him a hard look. 'I sometimes think I might have made an error in confiding in you too much,' he snapped. 'Just remember, you do pretty well with your cut on what we make out of those rustled cows and don't go shootin' your mouth off. I never liked too much loose talk.'

The marshal shuffled uncomfortably. 'Sure,' he said. 'I didn't mean anythin'. You know you can count on me.'

Brandon continued to stare at the marshal but then his features suddenly relaxed.

'That's fine,' he said. 'Just so long as we understand each other.'

Braithwaite realized the time had come for him to make a move. 'Thanks for the drink,' he said. 'I'd best be goin'. Just leave Seaton to me. The job's as good as done.'

'You will have my boys along to make sure it is,' Brandon replied. He gestured to the marshal to resume his seat. 'It's gettin' late,' he said. 'Why don't you stay over? There isn't any rush and there are spare places in the bunkhouse.'

The marshal would have preferred to be on his way, but didn't want to do anything that might go counter to Brandon's new-found affability.

'Sure,' he said.

'Have a word with Held. Make it a chance to get to know each other before you start workin' together. I'll see you in the mornin' before you go.'

The marshal walked to the door and made his way outside where he paused for a few moments, cursing under his breath, before making his way to the bunkhouse.

It was late at night as Seaton and Utah arrived in Lindenberg and made their way stealthily to the Sheepmen's Association building. The street was dark and all the other stores were closed. There was a narrow path at the side of the building and they led the horses down it to an overgrown lot with a battered shed at the rear, overlooked by trees.

'Ideal,' Seaton said. 'There's grass and nobody would be likely to see anythin' unless they deliberately sought it out.'

When they had made the animals comfortable they took a good look at the back of the building, seeking for a means of entry. The door was locked but one of the windows was smashed and it wasn't too difficult to remove the few splinters that remained and then climb through. Once inside, they stood in darkness, listening. There was a steady ticking noise that unnerved them for a moment till Seaton remembered the clock. He struck a match and they picked their way forward. The room was empty but at the far end he recognized the few items of furniture and the empty coffee cups he had seen when he had peered through the front window on his previous visit. A little more light entered from the street and he blew out the second match he had lit.

'It's not likely anyone would see, but there's no point in taking the chance,' he said, peering into the darkness. In a corner there was a door and Seaton opened it to find it led into a small entrance way with a stair winding up into the gloom. He began to climb the steps. At the top there was a passage with three doors leading from it, and when he opened them it was to find each room empty like the one below except for some scattered items of lumber. He heard a sound behind him and jumped as Utah came along the landing.

'Kinda spooky,' the oldster said.

'Yeah.'

'It's funny, but I never feel that way when I'm out in the open. It doesn't matter how dark or lonesome a place is; as long as the sky's over my head I don't mind.'

'We don't have to stay here long,' Seaton replied.

'I don't know about you, but I'm plumb tired. I figure I'll spread my blanket and try to get some shuteye.'

'Me too,' Seaton replied.

'Upstairs or down?' Utah asked.

'Down,' Seaton replied.

Without further ado, picking their way slowly, they descended the creaking stairs.

CHAPTER FIVE

Seaton and Utah managed to make themselves quite comfortable and they awakened to the early morning sounds coming from the street outside. Seaton crept to the window and peered out. The man opposite was sweeping the boardwalk outside his store with a broom and there were indications of people moving about further up the street towards town. Hearing a sound behind him, he turned away to face the oldster.

'I could use somethin' to eat,' Utah said.

'So could I,' he replied.

'I guess we're gonna have to be real careful when it comes to cookin'. At least we got some jerky and cold beans.'

Seaton turned back to where the daylight was beckoning.

'Hell,' he said, 'I want somethin' better than that. And I don't fancy stayin' cooped up here for too long.'

The oldster gave a gap-toothed grin. 'Me neither,'

95

he replied. He clutched at his stomach and added, 'Anyway, I'll see you in a few minutes. I'm just taking a little trip out the back.'

'Right. While you're doin' that, I'll take a look through some of those drawers.'

'You think you might find somethin'?' Utah asked.

'I don't know. It's one reason for comin' here, but I guess probably not. It might help if I had an idea what I'm lookin' for.'

The oldster stumbled away and, with a last glance outside, Seaton turned to the drawers. They were unlocked but his examination was fruitless. Moving the dirty coffee cups, he sat on the edge of the desk to think. He had not really been expecting to find anything, but had vaguely hoped there might be some trace as to the identity or whereabouts of the man Brown. He had been thinking of what Utah and the owner of the carpentry shop across the street had told him, and he was becoming more conscious of the role that Brown might have to play. It was a pretty safe bet that whoever had driven him away was also responsible for the attack on the oldster. He was sure now that it was Nash Brandon and his Mill Iron outfit, but proving it would be difficult. Brown could prove a crucial witness, but who was he and, more to the point, where was he? He racked his brains for an answer and then suddenly light dawned. All the time it was staring him in the face. He recalled what the carpentry shop owner had said about having seen the man leave in the company of Braithwaite. He had assumed it was because of some sort of legal nicety that needed sorting out, but Seaton realized that wasn't the case at all. In reality, the marshal had placed the man under arrest and was taking him away. In all probability he was now languishing in the jailhouse – unless something worse had happened to him. Just then he heard the shuffle of feet and looked up to see the oldster returning from his ablutions.

'That's better,' he said. 'Did you find anything?'

'Nope, but I think I know where we might find Brown.' Utah's eyes opened wide. 'I figure he's locked up in Braithwaite's jailhouse,' Seaton concluded, 'and if he is, we've got to come up with a way of gettin' him out of there.'

Marshal Braithwaite could have done without the services of Brandon's two ranch-hands, and he thought he knew a way of getting them out of his hair. When they arrived in Lindenberg and stabled their horses at the back of the marshal's office, he walked with them to the Exchange Hotel. Telling them to wait outside, he entered the lobby and approached the clerk at the reception desk. The clerk gave him a worried look.

'I'm making further enquiries about the man Seaton,' Braithwaite said. 'Has he returned to his room yet?'

'No. I haven't seen him.'

'Let me have his key.'

The receptionist hesitated a moment before complying. He didn't like doing it, but reflected that, after all, it was the marshal, the representative of law and order, who was asking him. The marshal took the key and made for the stairs. Seaton's room was the first door on the landing and he stood outside for a moment, listening, before turning the key and looking inside. The clerk was right. The room was empty. He didn't even stop to look around but, locking the door, made his way back to the lobby.

'Thanks,' he said. 'If Mr Seaton shows up, be sure to let me know.' He went outside where Held and his companion were waiting.

'Seaton isn't here,' he said, 'but he could return at any time. I want you two boys to keep a close watch on the place. Take a room if you want – I'm sure Mr Brandon wouldn't mind since he owns it. If you see Seaton, you know what you have to do.'

'What about you, Marshal?' Held asked.

'Don't concern yourselves about me. Just make sure to keep me informed.'

Without waiting for a reply, Braithwaite turned and walked away. Held and his companion watched his departing figure.

'Well,' Held said, 'I guess we should do as he says. We might as well get somethin' out of this.'

The marshal glanced back once to see them disappearing into the hotel before continuing on his way to the Blue Front saloon. Having got rid of them for the time being, he needed some refreshment.

It was later in the afternoon and he was back in his office carrying on where he had left off at the saloon when there was a knock on the door and it opened to reveal an elderly man carrying a tray draped with a cloth. He looked at the man with a puzzled expression on his face.

'Who the hell are you and what have you got there?' he said.

'Food for the prisoner,' the man replied.

A frown creased Braithwaite's brow. 'This ain't the time. I didn't order anythin'.'

'I don't know about that. I'm just carryin' out instructions.'

Braithwaite looked at the man closely. 'Come here,' he said. 'Let's see what's on that tray.'

The man walked over to the marshal and lifted the drape. There was a plate with bacon and beans and a mug of coffee.

'I reckon I could use that myself,' the marshal said. 'Where did it come from?'

'The café across the way.'

'The Broadway café?'

'Yup. Is it OK to take it through?'

The marshal's brain was more than a little bemused by drink. 'Who told 'em I'm holdin' a prisoner?' he asked.

'Like I say, I don't know nothin'. I'm just a delivery boy.'

Braithwaite considered the matter for a few moments longer before shaking his head. 'Take it back, he said. 'The prisoner don't get anythin' to eat till I say so.'

The man shrugged. 'Whatever you say,' he replied. 'It don't make any difference to me.'

He shuffled his way out, closing the door behind him. The marshal continued to sit with a frown on his face before eventually finishing off his drink and pouring himself another.

Seaton, watching anxiously out of the window of the Broadway café, felt himself relax a little when Utah came out of the marshal's office, carrying the tray. The oldster crossed the road and entered the café. The café proprietor, a buxom woman of a certain age, looked up as the door closed behind him.

'Marshal Braithwaite changed his mind?' she said.

'He doesn't seem to be in a good mood,' the oldster replied. 'Seems a pity to waste good food. I guess I'll just have to eat it myself.' The woman chuckled and Utah seated himself next to Seaton.

'Well?' Seaton asked.

'You're right. Braithwaite's definitely holdin' a prisoner back there. But it's still not certain it's Brown.'

'Maybe not, but I'm willin' to take the chance. What else did you find out?'

'The keys are hangin' from some pegs right behind his desk. And you're in luck. The door to the cells is in the right-hand corner and it's standin' slightly ajar.'

'There's no one else? No deputy marshal?'

'Nope, leastways not at the moment. He's on his own.'

Seaton's jaw tightened. 'OK,' he said. 'That's good enough for me. Don't waste any time finishin' those beans. When I come out of there, be waitin' by the horses ready to ride.'

With a nod in the direction of the lady proprietor, he left the café and strode purposefully across the street.

Reaching the marshal's office, he threw the door open and stepped inside with his six-gun in his hand, kicking the door shut behind him.

'What the hell!' the marshal exclaimed. He rose partly to his feet when he recognized the intruder.

'Seaton!' he gasped, and after a second's pause, added, 'I'm lookin' for you.'

'Then it seems like you found me.'

'What do you want? You know you're committing a serious offence threatenin' a man of the law?'

'Less of that stuff about bein' a man of the law. I know you, Braithwaite, and you've got it comin' to you.'

Braithwaite's demeanour suddenly changed and he took a step backwards.

'Unbuckle your gun belt and throw it on the floor,' Seaton snapped.

Braithwaite didn't respond at first and Seaton had to repeat the command before he tremblingly complied.

'Get the key to the cells,' Braithwaite ordered. Again Braithwaite hesitated.

'I said get the key to the cells and make it quick!' Seaton rapped.

Braithwaite turned, took a step and reached for the key, after which he looked pleadingly at Seaton.

'OK, let's go!' Seaton said.

The marshal didn't move and Seaton prodded him with the gun. They made their way to the door at the back of the office, which stood slightly open as Utah had said. On the other side of it a short corridor led through to the back where there were two cells standing side by side. In one of them a man stood with his hands clutching the bars.

'Is your name Brown?' Seaton rapped.

The man nodded his head. It was only when he got close to him that Seaton noticed his face was bruised and there was a cut above his right eyebrow. He looked bemused and Seaton tried to reassure him before turning back to the marshal.

'Open the door and go inside,' Seaton said.

The marshal's initial bravado had evaporated but he summoned up one last ounce of resistance.

'You won't get away with this,' he said, and then, rather feebly, 'this is against the law.'

'Just do it,' Seaton replied. The marshal's hands were shaking and it took him a few moments to open the cell door.

'OK, give me the key and swap places.'

Brown came out of the cell, looking as bemused as the marshal. Braithwaite held back for a moment and Seaton pushed him in, locking the door.

'Don't make any noise,' Seaton told Brown. 'Not if you want to stay alive.' Without more ado he took Brown's arms and steered him along the corridor and into the marshal's office.

'What's happening?' he managed to say.

'Don't worry. We're on your side, but the explanations will have to wait.'

He stepped to the door and, opening it, glanced up and down the street. Things were quiet; a little way down he could see Utah holding the horses by a hitching rail.

'OK,' he said to Brown. 'Just act normal. There are three horses a little way along the main street. We'll make our way to them.'

Still holding Brown's arm, he ushered him out of the office and into the sunshine. Brown blinked and screwed up his eyes but offered no resistance. In a matter of moments they had reached the horses and, climbing into leather, they began to ride away. Seaton was just congratulating himself on a job well done when he saw a flash of light and a bullet went singing through the air, rapidly followed by another. He couldn't make out who was doing the shooting, but the response was quick as, following his lead, they all broke into a gallop. They thundered down the street, the noise of their horses' hoofs drowning out the sound of gunshots, and soon they had left the town behind. They slowed down but carried on riding till they were well clear when, at a signal from Seaton, they drew to a halt.

'Who was that throwin' the lead?' Utah asked.

'I don't know. Somebody must have recognized us.' Seaton turned to Brown, who was looking quite shaken.

'You must be wonderin' what all this is about,' he said. Quickly, he introduced himself and Utah and outlined the situation. When he had finished Brown seemed to have gathered his wits.

'Well,' he said, turning to Utah, 'I never expected to meet you under these circumstances, but it's nice to see you again. From what you and Mr Seaton have just told me, it seems like I'm lucky to still be here at all.'

Seaton nodded. 'I reckon you're not far wrong, especially if you can confirm that it was Brandon and his boys who were responsible for closin' you down.' He looked again at Brown's face. 'Looks like you took a beating,' he added.

The man raised his hand and touched his bruised cheek. 'I'm fortunate they didn't do worse,' he said. 'You're right about Brandon. And it looks like the marshal is on his payroll too.'

'You'd better tell us just what happened.'

'There ain't a lot to tell. I knew I was takin' a chance settin' up the Sheepmen's Association and introducin' sheep to cattle country, but I wasn't expectin' this. I'd had a few warnings; I even had a visit from Brandon himself offerin' me money to move out. Maybe I should have taken him up on it. A few days ago Brandon's hardcases arrived and roughed me up. Then the marshal came. He accused me of causing a disturbance and put me in jail.'

Seaton took a long hard look at their back trail. 'We'd better carry on ridin',' he said. 'We can fill in the details later. I won't feel happy till we've put some distance between the marshal and us.'

'Where are we goin'?' Utah asked.

'The only place I can think of for the moment is your old line cabin,' Seaton replied.

He quickly explained the plan of action to Brown. 'By the way,' he added, 'is Brown your real name? We kinda figured you might have made it up.'

'I guess you're both right and wrong,' Brown replied. 'The name's Brownlow, Thadeus Brownlow. I guess changin' it was a bit of a pointless exercise on my part, but it seemed a reasonable idea at the time.'

'One other thing,' Seaton answered. 'Now things are kind of out in the open, would you be willin' to testify against Brandon?'

Brownlow thought for a moment. 'You think it might come to that?'

'We sure don't aim to let Brandon get away with all this,' Seaton replied. 'I don't know how it'll work out, but I figure to bring him to justice in a court of law.'

'You realize that Brandon is a big noise in the county? It'd be a tough job you're proposin' to take on.'

'Yeah, but that's all the more reason not to let him get away with ridin' roughshod over everyone.'

Brownlow looked from Seaton to Utah and back again. A smile spread slowly across his battered features. 'Well,' he said ruefully, 'I reckon you could definitely say that Brandon's rode roughshod over me. I'm just glad you boys have given me an opportunity to pay him back. I'm with you.'

Seaton and Utah exchanged glances and the oldster let out a muted yell. 'Jumpin' Jehosaphat! Brandon won't have a chance against the three of us.'

Seaton extended his hand and Brownlow took it. 'Good to have you on board,' Seaton said.

Without more ado, they set off in the direction of the Lazy Ladder. They rode at a steady pace, looking back from time to time to check that they were not being pursued. It was only a question of time till somebody discovered the marshal and released him, and Seaton reckoned it wouldn't take too long. He thought about the shots that had been fired at them. Who was it? If it was someone whose suspicions had been aroused by seeing him enter the marshal's office, it might take less time than he hoped for the pursuit to begin. As he reflected on the incident, it seemed to him that more than one man had been involved. Who stood to gain by killing them? Could it be anyone else but Brandon and the Mill Iron? And after all, there had already been an attempt on his life at the livery stables. Maybe it was the same people who were involved. If he had got wise to Brandon and his boys, Brandon in turn had got wise to him. The issue had become personal for him as well as them. In the wake of this conclusion, he somehow found himself thinking of Maisie Montgomery.

That same afternoon, Maisie Montgomery was sitting on the veranda of the ranch-house reading a book when she heard hoof beats and looked up to see her father approaching. She got up from her chair as he drew his horse to a halt and lowered himself from the saddle.

'Father!' she said. 'I didn't expect you back so soon.' She observed the worried look on his face. 'Is anything wrong?' she asked anxiously.

Mitch Montgomery took her arm as he came up the steps and drew her gently back into her seat while he lowered his tall, slightly stooping frame into another opposite.

'What are you reading?' he asked.

She held the book up for him to see the title. '*The Autocrat of the Breakfast Table,*' he read. 'Somehow I don't reckon that's gonna be one for the bunkhouse library when you've finished.'

'I'm sure some of the men would find it of interest.'

'Maybe, although I think they're more used to mail-order catalogues and stock journals.'

She put the book down on a stool and then looked up at him. 'You don't usually come back in the middle of the day,' she said, 'and I don't imagine you did so in order to talk about books.'

He shuffled uncomfortably in his chair before replying. 'I'm not sure how to put this,' he said, 'so I guess the best thing is to come straight out and say it. Just lately things haven't been goin' so well and I ain't sure I'll be able to meet all my commitments. If it wasn't for the way you handle the housekeepin' I figure I'd have gone under by now. Just lately I've been losin' stock too. The fact of the matter is, I've decided I'm gonna have to sell the Lazy Ladder.'

He stopped to see her reaction. It wasn't what he had expected.

'Sell the Lazy Ladder,' she said, repeating his words. 'You can't do that! It's our home. I don't want to live anywhere else. There must be something we can do? I'll take a job – maybe teach school or work in one of the stores.' She paused. 'Have you had an offer for the Lazy Ladder?' she asked.

'As a matter of fact, I have.'

'Is it from Nash Brandon and the Mill Iron?'

He glanced at her in surprise. 'How did you know that?' he asked. 'I don't recall ever mentioning it.'

She smiled and gently shook her head. 'You're not very good at hiding things,' she said. 'But then why are you telling me this now?'

'Because I'm going into town this afternoon to have a word with Brandon's lawyer about setting up a meeting.'

For a few moments her brow was puckered in thought. 'Don't do that,' she said. 'If you've put off selling the Lazy Ladder all this time, it can wait a few more days.'

'What good would that do? I'm about at breakin' point. One more thing and I'll be over the edge and then I might have to sell at a lower price than I'm likely to get now.'

'Just wait. I'll think of something.'

He smiled forlornly. 'I'm sorry to have to do this. I know how much you love the Lazy Ladder. But what else can I do? We'll find somewhere else.'

'No we won't. There'll never be anywhere else like the Lazy Ladder. I don't want you to sell it, and least of all to Nash Brandon. I don't like him. I told you what that man Seaton had to say when he visited the ranch. He said something about an attack on a friend of his and I'd be willing to bet that Brandon was behind it. He's probably responsible for stealing your stock.'

'Now that's not fair. I never said anything about stealin'. I said I'd been losin' some stock. When we carry out the roundup they'll probably turn up.'

'I still don't like Brandon. I'd be willing to bet he's not offering you a fair price either.'

'There, that's enough,' her father replied. He thought for a moment. 'I don't want to announce any of this without giving the men time to take it in and make arrangements about what they're gonna do. That wouldn't be fair.' He bit his lip, his troubled brow puckered in thought.

'OK,' he said at last. 'I'll give it a few more days, but I don't see any way out.'

She leaned over to him and flung her arms about his neck. 'Oh, thank you. I'm sure something will turn up. I won't let it happen. I'll think of a way. Just have faith.'

He kissed her on the brow and got to his feet. 'I'd better get on,' he said.

'Will you be in your study?'

'For a while. I've got some paperwork to do.'

'I'll bring you some coffee,' she said.

He went through the ranch-house door and she continued to sit forward on her chair, looking out across the yard and away into the distance. The familiar scene seemed to have acquired a new poignancy and a new meaning. It wasn't possible that she should lose it and the Lazy Ladder become incorporated into some bigger spread, but what was to be done about it she couldn't tell.

Seaton had suggested the line cabin as a place of refuge, but he knew it could only be temporary and he needed to decide on a proper plan of action. When morning came he still hadn't decided on what it should be. Normally, he would have approached the marshal with his concerns, but Braithwaite was one of Brandon's creatures and there was nothing to be looked for in that direction. As Utah and Brownlow tended to the horses, he stood in the doorway, racking his brains for an answer, when he spotted something in the distance; a smudge or stain against the sky.

'Hey!' he called. 'Come and take a look.' Utah and Brownlow came round a corner of the cabin.

'What is it?' Brownlow asked.

'Could be dust,' Utah replied. 'Or maybe it's Braithwaite with a posse!'

They stood observing it closely till Seaton suddenly exclaimed, 'That ain't dust. That's fire!'

There was a moment's hesitation and then with one accord they grabbed their saddles and some sheets and made their way to the horses. As they rode out, the smear of smoke had already grown to a cloud, which quickly gathered in density and expanded as they got nearer. Some cattle came tearing towards them, veering off while they were still some distance away, and then Seaton noticed another line of smoke coming from a different direction. At first he thought the fire had jumped and spread, but when he detected horsemen he guessed that they had deliberately started a backfire and were driving it towards the flames ahead of them. Although the main fire was still some distance away, they could hear the crackling and roaring of the flames as they got closer and the heat made the air dance in front of them. There were two lines of smoke now advancing across the grass and gradually coming together, and through the smoke the red glow of the blaze flickered and flared, sending sparks flying high into the air.

The men fighting the fire were too involved to take notice of the new arrivals as they came alongside and made towards a chuck-wagon that was coming up behind carrying water barrels. Taking the sheets they had brought, they soaked them with water and, abandoning their horses, advanced to join in the battle. Where enough space had been burned to prevent the grass on the leeward side of the backfire from igniting, they moved on down the sides to stop the fire from breaking over at other places. They worked tirelessly, but it was clear that more men were needed and the supply of water was inadequate. Their sheets were soon burned and they replaced them with gunny sacks, riding back to the wagon regularly to dip them into one of the barrels. Around them the *thud thud* of the wet sacks could be heard above the crackling of the flames, leaving behind black ashes and little streamers of smoke where they'd struck. As they beat out fresh blazes with the water-soaked sacks, they left trails of smouldering

111

black which as often as not were fanned into new life by the breeze and sparks falling on the dry grass. All the while the backfire was forced to burn slowly into the breeze, but it was very questionable as to whether, when it met the oncoming fire, they would then burn themselves out.

The lines of fire drew closer together, and as the men toiled thick billows of pungent smoke blew into their faces. Flakes of blackened grass and ashes settled on them and the air was thick with cinders. Sparks danced among the smoke. The heat of the fires beat upon them, scorching their faces and making their eyes sting and smart. The hot ground was baking the horses' hoofs as showers of soot fell over them and the smell of burning grass and sage-brush, weeds and cow chips, filled the air. The men's faces were soon black and blistered. Seaton found it hard to keep track of what was happening to Utah and Brownlow as they continued to labour.

Someone had ordered the killing of a couple of steers. They had been sliced in half, their heads cut off and their sides skinned from belly to back, and then they were pulled along behind the chuck-wagon. The idea was to drag the carcases by their front and hind legs over the edges of the blaze to help extinguish the flames, but looking ahead at the conflagration it seemed a hopeless response. Still they struggled on but despite all their efforts, other fires kept breaking out behind them and there was a growing danger that they might be encircled. The dense smoke made it hard to see what was happening but as Seaton came through a dense patch he saw a man a little way in the rear of the drags, lying prone on the smouldering ground and almost surrounded by the dancing flames of one of the secondary fires.

Weighing up the situation in an instant, he ran towards the conflagration. Holding the wet sack in front of him for protection, he aimed his run at a spot where the flames were less fierce. He crouched low in an effort to protect his face and with a final leap he was through. The man lay face down and as tongues of flame reached towards him, Seaton kneeled down and turned him over. The man's face was scorched and he was barely breathing but he was still alive. Quickly, Seaton wrapped him in the wet blanket with which a few moments before he had been trying to douse the flames and then lifted him as carefully as he could. The man was heavy and the effort involved almost exhausted him. His lungs felt as though they were on fire from the smoke and cinders he couldn't help breathing in. Desperately, he looked about for a way of escape and then, gathering all his remaining strength, he put the man over his shoulder and staggered forward. He was no longer in full control of himself, but acting by instinct as he shouldered his way through the flames to emerge at the other side blind and disoriented. He made a few more steps before collapsing to the ground with his burden. He got to his knees, his head down, gasping for air, and was barely aware when a couple of men came to his assistance. He looked up into their faces and saw their mouths move and tried to tell them what had happened before collapsing in a welter of pain and exhaustion.

He was awakened by a jolting motion to find himself lying on the bed of the chuck-wagon and looking down at him were the faces of Utah and Brownlow. He attempted to move but Utah restrained him with a gentle touch.

'Take it easy,' he said.

'I feel like hell,' he managed to reply.

'That ain't no surprise,' Utah said. 'You were damn lucky to come out of the fire at all, never mind carryin' somebody else with you.'

'You know you're somethin' of a hero?' Brownlow said. 'Turns out that man you risked your life to rescue is Mitch Montgomery, the owner of the Lazy Ladder.'

'Is he OK?' Seaton asked.

'He ain't too grand, but he'll survive.'

Seaton managed a feeble grin as a third face came into view behind those of Utah and Brownlow.

'Seaton,' Utah said, 'this here is Lem Hillier. He's foreman at the Lazy Ladder.'

Seaton looked at him but it was difficult to make out much of his features beneath their smearing of soot and ash.

'How are you feelin'?' he asked.

'Pretty bad, but I'll be OK.' He made another effort to sit up and despite Utah's remonstrances, succeeded in hoisting himself upright. Hillier was riding his horse close to the chuck-wagon, in which another figure was lying whom he recognized as the man he had rescued.

'We sure owe you,' Hillier said. 'Without you, Mr Montgomery wouldn't be here.'

'Think nothin' of it.'

'We're gonna let the fire burn itself out now. I don't think we can do a lot more and I don't want to take the risk of somebody else bein' hurt.'

Seaton raised his head to look over the side of the wagon and directed his gaze to the line of smoke which still hung in the distance.

'You figure we've done enough?' he said.

'I reckon so.' Hillier looked at Utah and Brownlow. 'Thanks to all of you,' he said. 'We were short-handed and you sure helped to pull us through.' He paused in thought for a moment. 'The main danger would be the threat to the ranch-house, but I think we've avoided any chance of it reachin' that far.'

His words suddenly made Seaton think of Maisie Montgomery and immediately evoked a worried response. What if the foreman was wrong? What if she had somehow been caught up in the blaze? He was relieved when Hillier continued, 'We're headed back there right now. We've already sent for the doc so he can check you out properly later. You're welcome to stay as long as you need.'

Seaton exchanged glances with Utah and Brownlow. Utah's face was blank but Brownlow nodded as if in approval. Seaton couldn't think of a better option. Their tenure of the line cabin had been a temporary expedient and it was unlikely they would be able to deal with Brandon on their own. They needed support if their cause was to be successful, and Mitch Montgomery seemed the obvious choice, especially after what had just happened. At some point they would have had to approach the Lazy Ladder, and events had turned out propitiously. From one point of view the circumstances were perhaps not ideal, but from another they had worked in their favour.

'Sure,' he said. 'That's real friendly of you. We appreciate it.'

'Good,' Hillier said. 'Just try and relax. I'll see you later after we get back to the ranch.' He was about to turn his horse and ride off when Seaton asked, 'What do you think started the fire?' He was expecting a quick reply, but instead Hiller took a few moments to consider.

'That's a good question,' he said, 'but range fires are not unusual. There are plenty of things it might have been.'

'You don't sound too sure.'

'We can maybe talk about that later but right now you ought to be restin'.'

He wheeled away and for the following moments Seaton and his two companions watched the fire. It had certainly diminished. The flames were beginning to die away and be replaced by a wall of billowing black smoke. It seemed that Hillier knew his business. At one stage it had looked like a losing fight, but they had succeeded in bringing the conflagration under some kind of control.

'Hillier didn't sound too sure about what caused the fire,' Utah commented.

'You noticed that too?' Seaton replied.

'I figure he's as suspicious as you are,' Utah replied. 'I wonder if it's Brandon and the Mill Iron he's got in mind too?'

Seaton lay back again. After Hillier had gone, he began to question himself as to why the foreman hadn't asked any questions about what they were doing on Lazy Ladder range in the first place. He wondered for a moment what the response would have been if they had been found on Mill Iron property, and he thought he knew the answer.

CHAPTER SIX

A couple of days had gone by and Seaton had seen nothing of either Mitch or Maisie Montgomery. It was easy enough to understand why Mitch wasn't around but Seaton was somewhat disappointed not to have seen Maisie. He consoled himself with reflecting that her time would be fully occupied looking after her father. He himself had been given a room upstairs in the ranch-house, whereas Utah and Brownlow had to make do with the bunkhouse. However, they were able to come and go quite freely and they spent a considerable amount of time in Seaton's company. After all the excitement and exertions of the previous few days, all three of them were glad of a chance to take time to rest and recuperate. However, Seaton didn't like the feeling of being treated like an invalid and despite some discomfort, made a point of being up and about as soon as possible. So when Hillier paid Seaton a visit the day after the fire to report that it had burned itself out, he took advantage of the opportunity to suggest they take a ride out and look at the damage.

'Are you sure you're up to it?' Hillier asked.

'Sure,' Seaton answered. 'The doc's given me a clean bill of health.'

'I'm not sure that's quite what he said,' Brownlow remarked.

The foreman looked at him dubiously. 'That's not what he said to Mr Montgomery either,' he said.

'That's Montgomery, this is me,' Seaton replied. 'He had a worse time of it than me. Stop fussin'. A bit of fresh air will do me good.'

They made their way to the corral where Seaton was pleased to see the chestnut looking in good shape.

'Hello, old girl,' he said, stroking her mane and muzzle. 'It takes more than a bit of smoke and fire to put us out of action.' They saddled up and left, Utah and Brownlow riding two cow horses from the remuda. As they rode, they began to notice the acrid smell of burned grass and as they got near the site of the fire they saw the whole range black and still smouldering in places in blue wisps of smoke. The smell had now become a stench and was strong in their nostrils.

'That's a lot of lost forage,' Seaton remarked.

'Yeah, and I don't think I'm sayin' anythin' out of line when I tell you the Lazy Ladder is already in difficulties.'

'When I asked you about what you thought started the blaze, you didn't seem too sure.'

Hillier gave the three of them a searching look.

'And you didn't say what you were doin' on Lazy Ladder property. Don't get me wrong. We're sure grateful for everythin' you did, but if things had been different, I might have had my suspicions.'

Seaton turned to Utah. 'Tell him what you saw,' he said.

'About the rustlers?'

Seaton nodded and in clipped sentences Utah described what had happened the night he sought shelter in the line cabin. When he had finished Hillier nodded and mumbled something under his breath, which Seaton couldn't make out.

'That ties in,' he said out loud. 'We've been losin' cattle for some time. I even set up some patrols but we haven't managed to catch anybody.' He paused.

'Go on,' Seaton prompted.

'I guess I don't have to spell it out to you. I figure you've worked it out for yourself. The way I see it, that fire was started deliberately, and by the same varmints who've been runnin' off our stock.'

'Yeah. That's the way we see it too. So who's behind it? I figure you've got a view on that too.'

Hillier gave a brief grin. 'Do you?' he said.

'Sure. And I got reasons.'

Hillier looked at him searchingly and Seaton took up the story where Utah had left off, starting with the attack on the oldster and his sheep and finishing with the rescue of Brownlow from Braithwaite's jailhouse and their subsequent night spent at the line cabin. When he had finished there was a knowing look on all their faces.

120

'Nash Brandon and the Mill Iron,' Hillier stated, saying it for them all. 'He's been tryin' to get his hands on the Lazy Ladder for a long while. I figured he was crooked, but it's worse than I allowed.'

'The question is, what do we do about it?' Utah said. Hillier regarded the oldster before replying.

'Brandon can't be allowed to get away with this,' he muttered. 'Leave it to me to tell Mr Montgomery, when he's recovered, what you just told me. I don't think he has any illusions about Brandon, but this puts everythin' in a new light. He's a quiet man, but I reckon we'll see a different side of him when he knows what's been goin' on.'

Marshal Braithwaite was in a state of high dudgeon when he was eventually set free from his own jail. A small group of people had gathered in his office, amongst whom he recognized Held and Thurston.

'What the hell are you all doin' here?' he yelled. 'Get out! Now!'

One or two people had shown concern, but at his words they didn't wait to offer their commiserations. When they had made their way outside again, Braithwaite accosted the two Mill Iron men.

'I thought I told you two to keep a close lookout for Seaton,' he fumed.

Held could see that he felt humiliated and was looking for someone to blame and decided the best response would be to try and justify themselves.

'We saw him comin' by and opened fire but he was travellin' too fast. It happened real quick, but at least

121

we recognized him. Who knows; we might even have wounded him.'

'Did he slow up? Did he look like he was hit?'

Held slowly shook his head. 'Nope, but that don't say he wasn't hurt.'

'I've heard about you two from Brandon,' the marshal said. 'If he was goin' to saddle me with somebody, I don't know why it had to be you.'

He sank into a chair, opened a drawer and produced a half-empty bottle of whiskey and a tumbler. He poured himself a stiff drink but didn't offer any to the other two. He gulped down a couple of mouthfuls and when he had done so he seemed slightly mollified.

'Right,' he said. 'This is what we do. This Seaton hombre obviously has some kinda connection with the Lazy Ladder. There's the horse at the livery stable for a start. I reckon there's a good chance that's where he and that no-good sheepherder are likely to be headed, so tomorrow or as soon as I can put a posse together we ride right on over there and bring 'em both in. And if either or both of 'em somehow get shot in the process, so much the better.'

Held sensed an easing of the atmosphere and attempted a smile. 'Whatever you say,' he replied. 'You're the boss.'

'I take it you're both stayin' at the Exchange Hotel?' Braithwaite said.

'Yes,' Thurston replied. Feeling it was too curt, he opened his mouth to add something but the marshal cut in.

'Make sure you're ready when I send for you.'

'We'll be ready,' Held said. Feeling the time was ripe to make an exit, he got to his feet and the other man followed his example. They both nodded at the marshal and made for the door.

'Don't let me down again,' the marshal snapped.

Held wasn't sure that they had done anything to let the marshal down in the first place, but Braithwaite was acting under Brandon's direction and he didn't feel in a position to raise any objections. Only when the two of them were safely out of the door did he turn to his companion and mutter, 'One day that low-down skunk is gonna get his come-uppance.'

The outcome of Hillier's talk with Mitch Montgomery was soon apparent. Seaton was leaning on a fence-post with Utah and Brownlow, looking over the horses in the corral, when the foreman appeared walking towards them.

'Well,' he said, 'I've been talkin' things over with Mr Montgomery, and I'm pleased to tell you he's right with us. I don't think he needed a lot of persuadin'. Anyway, the upshot is that he wants to meet up with you folks to offer his thanks personally and then discuss what needs to be done about Nash Brandon.'

Seaton swapped glances with Utah and Brownlow. 'That's great,' he said.

'How is Mr Montgomery?' Brownlow asked.

'He's fine. I've seen him look better, but he seems

to be more or less back to his old self. In fact, he'd like you boys to come over right now, if you've got nothin' else to do.'

'We're just fillin' in time,' Seaton said.

Hillier grinned. 'Come on then,' he said, 'let's not keep him waitin'.'

He led the way to the front of the ranch-house where a number of chairs were placed around a table on the veranda. Several people were already gathered, and Seaton felt a quickening of the pulse when he saw Maisie Montgomery among them. She arose at their arrival and put out her hand to Seaton as he came up the steps.

'Mr Seaton,' she said. 'I'm so glad to see you again. I'm only sorry I wasn't here to welcome you and your friends, but I've been away from the ranch. I only learned about what happened when I got back yesterday evening.'

Seaton had a feeling of relief at her words. He had assumed she was too busy caring for her father, but couldn't help a slight feeling of disappointment.

'No need to apologize,' he said. 'How is your father?'

His query seemed to slightly unsettle her. 'He's making a good recovery,' she replied. 'I have so much to thank you for. If you hadn't been there... '

'Please don't distress yourself,' Seaton replied. 'It seems to have all worked out for the best.'

'I should have been here. It was a mistake to leave the Lazy Ladder even for a few days but when I heard that a friend was ill, I thought it would be all

124

right to visit.'

'I'm sure she must have appreciated you makin' the effort.'

'It turned out to be nothing much really – just a mild fever. I should have left it to the doctor, but I wasn't to know.'

Seaton sensed her agitation and decided it might be sensible to change the subject by introducing his friends. When he had done so she appeared to have recovered something of her aplomb, and the situation was further diffused when the door to the ranch-house opened and Mitch Montgomery himself appeared. His face was burned and blistered, more so than Seaton's, and when he spoke there was a rasp to his voice.

'I see you've made our visitors welcome,' he said, addressing his daughter. 'Please, take a seat everyone. Help yourself to the refreshments.'

He lowered himself into a chair next to Seaton. 'I want to thank you for what you did,' he said. 'Without your bravery in coming to my assistance, I wouldn't have survived.'

'I don't know about that,' Seaton replied.

'It's true,' Montgomery said. 'And I want to thank your friends too. Your intervention was crucial. From now on, I hope you'll regard this ranch as a place where you will always receive a welcome.'

Utah and Brownlow muttered their thanks and then Montgomery turned to Seaton. 'Mr Hillier has told me what said. I feel you are all owed an apology for what you have been through.'

'None of it was your fault,' Seaton replied.

'Maybe not, but I still feel a responsibility for what happens in our little neck of the woods; and especially for the role played in all of it by Nash Brandon. There can be no question in my mind that he is directly responsible for your misfortunes as well as mine. More to the point, I think we can all agree that the time has come for us jointly to do something about it.'

Seaton glanced first at Utah and then at Brownlow.

'Well,' he said, 'I don't think any of us would disagree with you there. In fact, we were kinda countin' on your support.'

'Then let's drink on it,' Montgomery said.

They raised their glasses and had just put them down again when they heard the sound of hoof beats.

'Who can that be?' Montgomery asked.

They listened while the drum of hoofs grew louder and looked out towards the range. Presently a group of riders emerged, their horses kicking up a cloud of dust, and in the lead was Braithwaite. There were six others and they rode right up to the ranch-house before bringing their horses to a halt.

'Well, Marshal Braithwaite,' Montgomery said. 'This is an unexpected pleasure. It's real friendly of you to pay us a social call.'

The marshal's eyes flickered in Seaton's direction. 'This ain't no social call,' he said. 'This is business. I'm here to make an arrest.'

'Oh yes? That still doesn't explain what you're

doing here.'

'I'm here because the person in question is the man sittin' next to you.'

'These people are my guests,' Montgomery replied, 'and since you seem to be trespassing on my property, I'd advise you to turn right about and get the hell out of here.'

'And I'd advise you to co-operate, unless you want me to take you in as well for aidin' and abettin' a known outlaw.'

The marshal reached into an inside pocket of his jacket and produced some papers which he waved in front of Montgomery.

'Seaton,' he said, 'I have here a warrant for your arrest.' He turned to Brownlow. 'The same goes for you.'

'What's this gentleman accused of?' Montgomery asked.

'Jail breakin'. Evadin' the law. Assault. You need to be very careful, Montgomery, that you don't face the same charges.'

Montgomery smiled. 'Sorry, Marshal,' he said, 'but we can't oblige.'

'I don't want any trouble,' Braithwaite retorted. 'Just hand 'em over and we'll be on our way. Otherwise, I shall have to order my deputies to use force.'

There was a moment's tense silence. Seaton glanced at Maisie. Her features were set firm but he couldn't take a chance of her getting mixed up in any violence. He was about to indicate his compliance with the marshal's demands in order to defuse the situation when Montgomery spoke again.

'Braithwaite, you're nothin' but a two-bit skunk and you haven't got the guts to carry this through even with the help of your hired guns. Now I suggest you do like I just told you and ride away from here while you still got the option. And just in case you were thinkin' to push it any further, I think you'd better be made aware that I've got you and your boys covered. Some of my men have you in their sights. One false move and you'll be the first to die.'

Braithwaite licked his lips. Involuntarily, he lifted his eyes to glance at the windows of the ranch-house. Some members of the posse shifted uneasily in their saddles. Braithwaite made one more attempt at bluster.

'Just take it easy, Montgomery,' he said. 'No one wants any trouble. All you have to do is hand those two over and we'll be on our way. Think for a moment. They are wanted men. As the representative of law and order in Lindenberg, I would have thought I'd have your support in puttin' them behind bars.'

Montgomery's response was a dismissive laugh.

'You,' he said, 'you the representative of law and order.'

He got to his feet and walked to the top of the steps so that he stood on a level to Braithwaite, seated on his horse. For a moment they looked at each other eyeball to eyeball and then Montgomery quickly reached out his hand and tore the star from

128

the marshal's shirt. Briefly, he held it in his hand before throwing it into the dust of the yard. Braithwaite was taken by surprise and his immediate response was to reach for his gun but Seaton's Colt was already in his hand.

'I wouldn't think of doing that,' he said.

Braithwaite's face was twisted in anger and frustration but he realized that for the moment he was beaten.

'You ain't heard the last of this,' he snarled. 'We'll be back.'

With a word of command to the posse, he wheeled his horse and they all began to ride away, kicking up the dirt of the yard as they went. Montgomery stood watching them go until they were out of sight before turning to the others. There was a smile on his face and a glint in his eye.

'Well,' he said, 'that was unexpected but I think the marshal has been taught a lesson.'

Maisie rose from her seat and, rushing to him, put her arms around his neck.

'I'm so proud of you,' she said.

For a few moments they embraced before she withdrew and returned to her chair. Seaton slipped his gun back into its holster.

'You were taking a big risk bluffin' them like that, weren't you?' Hillier said.

Montgomery grinned. 'Take a look yourself,' he replied.

Hillier's face wore a puzzled look but he did as Montgomery had said, glancing into the ranch-house

129

windows. Behind each one was a man with a gun.

'It's the same upstairs,' Montgomery said. 'After what happened with the fire, I figured it might be as well to be prepared.'

Hillier grinned but his expression soon changed. 'I figure the marshal is gonna be real sore after havin' to climb down like he did,' he said. 'I gotta feelin' he's gonna be back soon with a bigger posse to back him up.'

'A posse includin' some of Brandon's hardcases, I wouldn't be surprised,' Seaton cut in. 'I agree with Hillier. We should prepare ourselves for a visit real soon.'

'Once Brandon realizes that his latest trick hasn't worked, he'll be more than ready to cast aside any pretence and launch an all-out attack,' Hillier added.

'We can't be sure that Brandon started the fire,' Maisie interjected.

'It might be hard to prove in a court of law,' her father replied, 'but has anybody got any doubts?' It was received as a rhetorical question, and the only response was a few grunts and a shaking of heads.

'If we're right and Brandon attacks the Lazy Ladder, we'll have our proof,' Utah remarked.

It seemed a good point and nobody added to it because just at that moment the door to the ranch-house opened and the cook appeared bearing a tray on which stood a big pot of coffee and some mugs.

'Sorry for the delay, Mr Montgomery,' he muttered. 'Seein' the marshal and his boys arrive kinda held things up a mite.'

'Thank you,' Montgomery said, 'and by the way, you did a good job getting that chuck-wagon with the water barrels to the fire so quick.'

'It was lucky I'd been gettin' things ready for the trail drive once we get those cow critters rounded up,' he replied.

Montgomery nodded. 'Yes,' he said, 'that's somethin' else we need to be thinkin' about.'

After leaving the Lazy Ladder, Marshal Braithwaite didn't return directly to town but instead made for the Mill Iron. He was still smarting from his encounter with Montgomery. He knew he had lost face with the posse and he was eager to waste no time in redressing the situation. To do that, Brandon's assistance seemed desirable. He had a feeling, too, that if he delayed and Brandon was to find out what had happened later, he would be in a particularly bad position. It seemed to him that his best chance of remaining in Brandon's good offices was to let him know exactly where Seaton and Brownlow were to be found. He could claim credit in having tracked them to the Lazy Ladder and he could give a suitable slant to what had just occurred. In his anger they rode too hard and eventually he had to slow down and then draw the posse to a halt in order to rest the horses, which were beginning to blow quite badly. As they sat their horses, Held rode up to him.

'Where are we goin'?' he asked. 'Someone was just sayin' we don't seem to be headin' back for town.'

'Who's sayin' it?' Braithwaite snapped.

131

Held paused before replying. 'Well, I guess we all are.'

Braithwaite's posse was hand-picked. He knew it was Held who was asking questions. Suddenly a new thought occurred to him.

'Well,' he said, 'since you're askin', I reckon the best place for you and your compadre to be headed is right back to the Lazy Ladder.' Held looked at him questioningly.

'As I recollect, Brandon assigned you two specifically to the task of gettin' rid of Seaton. Well, now you know where he is, you're in a position to do just that. And you can make an even better job of it by removin' Brownlow at the same time.'

'It'll be kinda risky now they've seen us,' Held replied.

'I doubt whether anyone took much notice of you two. But in any case, after the rustlin' and all, I would have thought you'd find it quite easy to stay un-noticed. All you have to do is just make yourself scarce and lie low till Seaton makes himself a target. He won't be expectin' anythin'. Hell, you'll be in and out of there before I've even had a chance to talk to Brandon.'

'You're headin' straight back for the Mill Iron?' Held replied. Without quite knowing why, Braithwaite wished he hadn't given away that piece of information.

'I'll let Brandon know what a good job you're doin',' he replied.

Held remained uncertain. Should he ignore the

marshal and keep on back to the Mill Iron? He didn't trust the marshal. He and Thurston were already in trouble with Brandon, and Braithwaite wasn't likely to present them in a good light. All in all, it might make sense to return to the Lazy Ladder and deal with Seaton. He wasn't so bothered about Brownlow. Braithwaite wasn't really asking a lot. All it needed was a little care. They had handled more difficult jobs.

'OK,' he said. 'We'll do it.'

'Good. And don't concern yourselves about Montgomery. Leave anythin' else to Brandon and me.'

Held muttered something in reply and then rode over to Thurston. They spoke together for a few minutes. Observing them, Braithwaite thought he detected a certain reluctance on the part of Thurston to go along with Held, but after another colloquy he seemed to be more amenable. He was expecting them to come over and say something to him, but without further ado they wheeled their horses and began to ride back the way they had come. Braithwaite turned to the other members of the posse.

'Come on boys,' he said. 'Let's get ridin'.'

It was getting late when Seaton bade goodnight to Utah and Brownlow. As the bunkhouse door closed on them, instead of making his way back to the ranch-house, he decided to take a stroll by the corral. It had been quite a day and it looked like there was to be a fight ahead, but for the moment the night was still and peaceful. The sky was thickly strewn with stars and a yellow moon hung low over the distant hills. The occasional stamp or snort of the horses only seemed to emphasize the tranquillity as he leaned on the corral fence and observed their shadowy forms. One of them came over, tossing its head, and he stroked its muzzle.

'Feelin' restless, old girl?' he whispered.

His voice sounded strange in the silent landscape. Suddenly he felt uneasy. He turned his head, looking all about him, before beginning to circle the corral, drawing his six-gun as he did so. A grove of trees stood at the back of the corral and he became aware of the soughing of the wind among their leaves. Still there was nothing he could see that might cause concern. Nonetheless his instincts were telling him to be careful, and over the years he had learned to trust them.

He stopped to look back at the ranch-house. The windows were dark except for one where a dim light glowed. He couldn't be sure, but suspected it was Maisie's room. What was she doing? Reading? Writing up her diary? He thought back to the events of the afternoon. She had shown no fear when the marshal and his stooges turned up and for a while it had looked dangerous. She was mainly responsible for the ranch functioning at all and she had certainly shown more determination than anyone in keeping it as a going concern. He turned away and was about to cross the short space of open ground between himself and the trees when the darkness was illumined by a stab of flame immediately followed by the crack of a rifle shot. He felt the wind of a bullet and immediately threw himself to the ground. Another shot rang out and a bullet thudded into a fence post inches above his head. The shot came from a different place among the trees so it was clear that more than one man was involved. At the sound of the explosions the horses in the corral took fright and began to whinny and rear; taking advantage of the confusion, Seaton crawled away to the shelter of some bushes.

He lay on his stomach, waiting for the next flash of flame. He heard a sound and looked back to see that Maisie's window was open. Praying that she wouldn't expose herself to danger, he turned his attention to the trees and was taken by surprise when he saw two figures emerge from the shadows. They were vague and indistinct and it was hard to tell whether they were moving away from him or towards him. He could only assume that they thought they had killed him. He might have fired from where he lay, but instead he leaped to his feet, calling out as he did so. He had some vague thought that he might catch them by surprise and they might throw aside their weapons, but their response was instantaneous as they opened fire and lead went singing through the night air. Going down again on one knee, he took a moment to take aim and then squeezed the trigger of his revolver. As the smoke cleared he saw the nearer figure crumple and fall. The other one began to run towards him, firing as he did so. Seaton triggered again and the man fell forwards, impelled by his own momentum before crashing heavily to the earth.

For a moment Seaton stood while silence descended, almost as unsettling as the noise of gunfire had been. Then he moved forward, knelt down and turned the man over. He was clearly dead. Seaton looked closely at his features but did not recognize him. He laid the man's head down on the ground and went to the other man. Blood was pouring from his mouth and from a wound in the chest. He was still alive but as Seaton tried to staunch the bleeding his eyes glazed and he was gone. This time Seaton thought he vaguely recognized him but he had no further chance to place him because a clamour had arisen from the ranch-house. Lights appeared and several people came running towards him with guns in their hands.

'Seaton, is that you?' a voice rang out.

He got to his feet and made haste to identify himself as they came up with Hillier in the lead followed by Utah and Brownlow. The foreman looked down at the two bodies lying in the dirt by the corral.

'What happened?' he snapped. 'Are you OK, Seaton?'

'I'm fine,' Seaton said. He gave a brief summary of what had just occurred.

'Hell,' Utah said when he had finished, 'you were lucky the outcome wasn't the other way round.'

Hillier looked around, his eyes peering into the

darkness. 'Come on,' he said, 'we'd better get inside, just in case there are any more of the varmints.'

'Hold on a moment,' Seaton said. 'I've got a feelin' I know one of 'em.' He kneeled down again beside the body of the man who had been shot in the chest.

'I'm sure I've seen him before somewhere,' he said.

Utah and Hillier leaned down to take a look and Hillier let out a muted exclamation.

'I reckon I know him too,' he said. 'His name is Held and he's one of Brandon's top men. I've come across him before in town.'

'That's it,' Seaton exclaimed. 'I can't be absolutely sure, but I reckon he's one of the men that tried to jump me at the livery stables.'

'In that case,' Hillier said, 'I think we've got all the proof we need that Brandon is our man. Not that we needed it.' He took another glance at the corpses. 'We can put 'em in a shed for now,' he said, 'and see about buryin' them tomorrow.'

They turned and were making their way towards the bunkhouse when Montgomery appeared.

'Sorry I got delayed,' he said, 'but Maisie was a little upset. She saw most of what happened from her window. Come over to the ranch-house. She's OK now and insisted on makin' some coffee.'

When they entered, she had already placed the coffee on the table. She looked up as they came in and Seaton couldn't help but notice that her anxious eye fell first on him.

'Mr Seaton,' she said, 'I saw what happened. Who were those men? Please tell me you're not hurt.'

'I'm fine,' Seaton replied.

She attempted to reply but there was a catch in her voice and with a murmured 'Excuse me', she turned and left the room.

'Today's events have unsettled her,' Montgomery said. 'She'll be perfectly all right. Who could use some coffee?'

They sat down and Montgomery poured. The hour was late and nobody had much to say. It was obvious to all of them that war had not only been declared, but they had just been involved in the first skirmish.

Braithwaite had intended heading directly for the Mill Iron, but after despatching Held and Thurston on their mission, he began to have second thoughts. Would it not be better to go back to Lindenberg and await developments? His mind was in a state of confusion and all he could do was to arrive at a compromise by sending the remaining members of the posse back to town and continuing on to the Mill Iron alone. Apart from anything else, he didn't want to take the risk of having to account for his tenure of his own cell. When they had left he continued riding for what seemed a long time. He was beginning to feel dozy and nodding in the saddle when he was brought to his senses by the appearance of a couple of horsemen riding rapidly towards him. He felt a sudden tension but relaxed as they got closer and he recognized them as Mill Iron ranch-hands.

'Howdy Marshal,' the first one said. 'Ain't you kinda out of your way some?'

'I didn't realize I was on Mill Iron range,' Braithwaite replied. 'As a matter of fact, I've come to see Mr Brandon.'

The man nodded. 'We'll ride right along with you,' he said. He turned to the other man who grinned. 'Just in case you get lost,' he added.

Braithwaite had no objections to them keeping him company, but he made a point of avoiding getting into conversation with them. Before long they arrived at the ranch-house, a long sprawling building with added wings and a covered walkway leading to the bunkhouse. Braithwaite dismounted while the other two rode away around the side of the building. Brandon must have seen them coming for he quickly appeared at the door.

'Marshal Braithwaite,' he said. 'I wasn't expecting a visit quite so soon. Won't you come on in?'

Braithwaite was feeling nervous and the sight of Brandon's large room with its costly furnishings and ornaments didn't serve to put him more at ease.

'You'll join me in a drink?' Brandon said, ushering him into a deep sofa.

Without waiting for a reply, he opened a cabinet, took out a bottle, and poured drinks for them both. He handed one to Braithwaite, adding, 'It's specially imported malt.'

Braithwaite took a sip. It tasted good, but no better to his palate than other whiskies he had tried.

'Well,' Brandon said. 'I don't suppose you've come all this way for the sake of your health. Is there something you want to tell me?'

Braithwaite took a larger swallow of the whisky and spluttered. He had been considering what would be the best way to put things, but any conclusions he had arrived at had gone from his head. Thinking that the best thing would be to limit his story to the bare essentials, he gave a brief account of how he had tracked Seaton to the Lazy Ladder.

'So what's he doing there?' Brandon asked.

'I don't know, but I thought you'd like to be kept informed.'

Brandon swilled the whisky in his glass and was thoughtful for a moment.

'You say Montgomery was there. How did he look? How did Seaton look, come to that?'

Braithwaite wasn't sure what Brandon was getting at, but Brandon provided the explanation himself.

'I don't know if you noticed anything, but my boys set his range on fire. Did a real good job of it too.'

'Now you mention it,' Braithwaite replied, 'I guess they did look a mite frazzled.'

Brandon burst into a laugh. 'Frazzled!' he repeated. 'Well, I guess that's one way of puttin' it.'

Braithwaite swallowed another mouthful of the whisky but didn't say anything. Brandon seemed to be in a good mood but he was treading carefully. Suddenly the rancher put his glass down and leaned forward.

'You say you set Held and Thurston to keep a

watch on things. Maybe they'll deal with Seaton and maybe they won't, but that's really beside the point now. My concern is with Montgomery. You'll agree I've made a good offer for the Lazy Ladder and given him every chance to sell. Well, it seems he's still not persuaded so I think the time has come to stop playing his little game and go ahead with playing mine instead.'

Braithwaite thought he understood what Brandon was saying and it seemed to tie in with his own aspirations.

'Are you sayin' you're plannin' to run Montgomery and his cowboys off the Lazy Ladder?' he said.

Brandon grinned. 'That's exactly what I'm saying, and I trust I have your support. Montgomery and his bunch of cowhands have been a constant source of trouble lately. Just look at what happened with the Sheepmen's Association. It's more than time for them to be brought to account and for law and order to be restored.'

'That's exactly the way I see it, Mr Brandon,' Braithwaite replied.

'Then I take it that I can count on your support and that I have the full backing of the law when I ride against the Lazy Ladder?'

'Sure thing,' Braithwaite replied. 'You can count on me up to the hilt.'

Brandon reached for his glass again. 'Then I say let's drink to puttin' Montgomery and the Lazy Ladder in their place once and for all.'

Braithwaite raised his glass and emptied the remaining contents, after which Brandon refilled it. By the time he had drunk another glass or two, Braithwaite was feeling good. All was right with the world after all. He and Brandon were brothers-in-arms, and his continuing role as marshal of Lindenberg was assured.

CHAPTER SEVEN

A day passed and then another without incident at the Lazy Ladder. There was work to be done in preparation for the roundup, but the men went about their business fully armed and on the lookout for trouble. It was a strange period of time. On the surface normality prevailed, but there was an underlying sense of tension because everyone knew an attack was likely. Montgomery and Hillier spoke about it to the ranch-hands, not trying to minimize the danger, but they all without exception accepted the situation and were ready to stand by Montgomery in the defence of the Lazy Ladder. That left one issue unresolved: what to do about Maisie. Montgomery's main concern was for the safety of his daughter, and after giving the matter a lot of thought he decided that the best course of action would be for her to move into Lindenberg, where she had friends with whom she could stay. What he hadn't reckoned on was her response to the suggestion, which was a polite but firm refusal.

'If Brandon does go on the offensive, the Lazy Ladder will be no place for a woman,' Montgomery pleaded.

She looked at him askance. 'When you came here and built up the ranch, who stood by you all the way?' she asked.

'I don't see what that has to do with it,' he replied.

'I know things weren't easy. You've told me yourself about how hard it was when you got started and the difficulties you had to face. It's not the first time you've had to face up to intimidation. You stood firm and you came through but you didn't do it alone.'

Montgomery grimaced. 'Your mother,' he said. 'She was right by my side.'

'Yes, she was. And were you really expecting me to behave differently? Now, of all times, when the chips are really down? You seriously imagined I'd creep away and hide myself in town?'

He looked at her and shook his head. 'No,' he said.

'If it does come to a fight,' she continued, 'I intend being right there in the thick of it. I can handle a gun as well as any man.'

'I don't know about that,' he said feebly.

'Well, I do.' She came close to him and put her head on his shoulder before raising her eyes to look into his face.

'We'll come through this together,' she said, 'the same as we always have. And Mother will be right there beside us too.'

He put his hands on her head and drew it gently

towards him to place a kiss on her brow.

'Yes, of course,' he said.

She smiled. 'Well, now that's settled,' she said, 'I've got chores waiting to be done. I'll see you later at supper.'

She withdrew from his touch and left the room, her dress making a swishing sound as she moved, while her father remained standing, the shadow of a smile playing around his lips. Her words had brought back a flood of memories, but he was presently aroused from his reverie by a knock on the door. Pulling himself together, he opened it to find Seaton and Utah standing outside.

'Sorry to disturb you,' Seaton said, 'but would it be OK if we had a word?'

'Of course. Come on in.' He stepped to one side as they entered and then closed the door behind them.

'Take a seat,' he said. 'Can I offer you a drink?'

Seaton waved aside the offer. 'We don't want to take up too much of your time,' he said.

'In that case, what can I do for you?'

Seaton paused for a moment before replying. 'Me and Utah have been thinkin',' he said. 'I reckon we're all agreed that there's a high chance of Brandon and his boys makin' an attack on the Lazy Ladder.'

'I should think that's certain,' Montgomery interrupted.

'Yeah. Well, that bein' the case, neither of us feel too happy about waitin' around for it to happen.' He glanced at Utah.

'We don't like the idea of bein' pinned down in the ranch-house,' the oldster confirmed. 'We both figure it would be handin' Brandon the advantage.' He chuckled grimly. 'Not that he ain't got it already.'

'In short,' Seaton concluded, 'we figure the best way to defend the Lazy Ladder would be by takin' the fight to Brandon.'

He stopped, wondering whether they might not have overstepped Montgomery's hospitality. After all was said and done, he was the boss and it was his fight, not theirs, but they needn't have worried. Almost before the words were out of his mouth, Montgomery's face creased in a grin.

'That's the way I feel too,' he replied. 'I've been giving it a lot of thought and it seems to me that it would be a mistake to let the men carry on waiting on events. It's bad for morale. We need to take the initiative. That's why I've already posted a couple of men to stand guard on the trail to the Lazy Ladder and let me know the instant they see any sign of Brandon and his men. If and when they do, we'll make sure we're ready to go out and meet them.'

Utah chortled. 'By Jiminy,' he said, 'seems like you're already one step ahead of us.'

Seaton was less effusive. 'I'd be happier still if we just aimed for the Mill Iron,' he said.

Montgomery grunted in assent. 'So would I,' he replied, 'but then we'd be puttin' ourselves in the wrong. We can't be absolutely sure about Brandon's intentions. I think we've got no choice but to let him make the first move.'

Seaton remained thoughtful for a moment and then nodded. 'You're right,' he said. 'But let's make sure that when we get the word, we're ready for the fight.'

'You can rest assured on that score,' Montgomery replied.

'Brandon won't be expectin' us to meet him in the open,' Utah concluded. 'He'll be taken by surprise. With any luck, we might catch him cold.'

Montgomery rose to his feet. 'Well,' he said, 'now we're all of one accord, I think we should have a drink after all.'

As Montgomery poured, he reflected that the conclusions at which they had arrived had the additional advantage of reducing the risk to Maisie's safety. Anything which might help to keep her out of the firing line was to the good. He wasn't the only one to think that way. Seaton, too, had his concerns and was feeling a little happier about the rancher's daughter.

On his return to Lindenberg, Marshal Braithwaite lost no time in reconstituting the posse and adding to it a few more of his cronies, advising them to be ready to ride at any time. He spent a good part of the rest of his time in his office, awaiting the summons from Brandon to join him at the Mill Iron prior to launching the attack on the Lazy Ladder. He was also half expecting Held and Thurston to return with the news that Seaton had been finally disposed of, but

when they didn't show up he wasn't unduly concerned. They meant nothing to him and he would be
quite happy if he never saw them again. In all likelihood, they had fouled things up the same way they
had done previously, and if Seaton had escaped their
murderous intentions, then so much the better. He
would welcome the chance of making Seaton pay for
the humiliation of being locked in his own cell. In
connection with that episode, he felt a grudge
against the proprietor of the Broadway café, who
seemed to have had some involvement. Since the
lady was popular in town and he had, in the past,
made tentative advances towards her, he decided in
the end to give her the benefit of his doubts and do
nothing about it, at least for the time being. Time
passed; he was beginning to grow restless and had
almost decided to ride out to the Mill Iron to check
things out when Brandon himself appeared.
Fortunately Braithwaite saw him coming and was
able to put away the bottle of whiskey and the
tumbler before the door was flung open and
Brandon burst through.

'OK, Braithwaite,' he said. 'Round up your boys
and be at the Mill Iron by noon tomorrow.
Everything's in place. It's time to deal with the Lazy
Ladder once and for all.'

It was a big bunch of riders that set out from the Mill
Iron. They were in good spirits; some of them yelled
and whooped as they rode away and others fired
their rifles into the air. Riding at their head along

148

with Marshal Braithwaite, Brandon felt a surge of excitement at the prospect of finally getting rid of Montgomery and taking the Lazy Ladder for his own. At the back of his mind was the titillating prospect of taking Maisie Montgomery too. The drumming of hoof beats stirred his blood and he felt a surge of pride and power made all the more thrilling by the reflection he was only at the beginning of what he meant to achieve. He felt like a conqueror and such was the general air of buoyancy that they rode a little faster than might have been prudent. Nobody was expecting Montgomery to put up much resistance, so as they approached the Lazy Ladder they were somewhat surprised to see, in the distance and obscured by dust, another group of horsemen approaching them. Brandon peered ahead.

'Who the hell is it?' he shouted to Braithwaite.

'I don't know!' the marshal yelled in reply.

There were indications of some uncertainty among the body of the riders and they all slowed. Braithwaite stared intently at the oncoming riders and as the dust raised by them cleared for a moment, finally recognized the owner of the Lazy Ladder.

'It's Montgomery!' he called.

Brandon had been expecting to take the Lazy Ladder by surprise and was momentarily disconcerted. Before he could respond, a voice behind him boomed some order and the posse burst forward once more, catching Brandon and the marshal in a tide of galloping horses. Shots were beginning to be fired and with a touch of bravado, Brandon belatedly raked his horse with his spurs. As it sprang forward, he took some comfort from the fact that Montgomery's party seemed to be a lot smaller than his own. All the same, as more shots boomed out, he didn't waste much time in tugging at the reins to restrain the eager beast.

For his part, Montgomery was quite happy for Brandon to come at him. To counteract the Mill Iron's charge, he ordered his men to take an opposite course and spread out to make themselves a more difficult target. Brandon's men bore down on them, firing as they rode. It wasn't very effective because they were moving too fast. Montgomery's response was more damaging as the bunched riders made an easier target. Some of their horses went down, throwing their riders and causing a degree of confusion behind. Montgomery and his men had formed a rough semi-circle, into the heart of which the Mill Iron horsemen rode, but as they met with a hail of bullets they began to break apart. Seaton's Winchester was hot in his hands as he pumped lead at the oncoming horde. Brandon's men were taking some heavy losses, but as they came into closer quarters the mass of riders began to break apart into separate groups. The Lazy Ladder men closed with them, and the struggle took on a desperate edge as each group fought hard to gain the upper hand. Seaton found himself facing an oncoming rider and drew the chestnut to one side, pressing the trigger of his Winchester as the man's horse went plunging by.

150

The man fell backwards and crashed to the ground. Almost immediately another horseman appeared; holding his rifle with one hand, he squeezed off another shot and the man fell away to the side. His foot caught in the stirrups, preventing him from falling cleanly, and his screams rang out above the tumult of battle as he was dragged along the ground. As he turned his mount to meet a further threat from his rear, a bullet ricocheted from the saddle horn and the chestnut reared. He was almost thrown, but managed to regain control at the cost of losing his rifle, which was shaken from his grasp. Reaching for one of his six-guns, he began to blaze away at the melee which had formed, but quickly realized that he was taking a risk of hitting one of the Lazy Ladder men.

A dense cloud of dust hung over the scene and it was hard to see what was happening. He felt a bullet tug at the sleeve of his jacket as he paused to jam more slugs into his revolver. Out of the melange of men and horses two riders appeared, galloping hard towards him. He raised his gun and fired and they veered off, heading away from the fray. There seemed to be a general movement backwards on the part of Brandon's men, and raising his head, he thought he detected the figure of Montgomery astride his horse, waving his arm as a signal to the others. As the Mill Iron riders slowly retreated, Montgomery's men advanced, spreading a heavy curtain of lead in front of them. Seaton had a definite feeling that Brandon's men were beginning to wilt. Their answering fire had dwindled and as the cloud of dust and smoke thinned, he saw some of them riding away. Suddenly he stiffened; among them he thought he recognized Braithwaite riding hard alongside another man astride a big palomino. The appearance of the horse was enough to tell him that the other rider must be Brandon. The fact that they were fleeing the scene could only mean that the tide of battle had definitely turned in Montgomery's favour and that Brandon, realizing the fight was lost, was trying to make good his escape. Instantly Seaton clapped his spurs to the chestnut's flanks and set off in hot pursuit.

The chestnut was a good horse and as it settled into its stride, Seaton began to close on his quarry. Brandon and the marshal were heading for the open country but suddenly they changed direction and began to ride towards the Lazy Ladder. Seaton's heart gave a jump. Maisie was waiting back at the ranch. He wasn't sure whether it was because they had seen him but the move had cost them a little more ground and he continued to gain on them. His horse stretched forward as he lay low in the saddle, seeming to relish the chase. If Brandon and the marshal had not seen him before, they were certainly aware of him now. Braithwaite turned and began to fire wildly with his six-shooter. It was a foolish move; there was little chance of a bullet finding its mark and it only served to slow them both down. In response, Seaton leaned further forward in the saddle to lessen the chances of being hit and to let the weight of his body assist the chestnut. As he rode, he kept a lookout for any other riders and at one point caught a glimpse of a horseman but he very quickly disappeared behind a rise in the ground. Despite his best efforts, Brandon and the marshal were still some distance ahead when the ranch-house came into view.

They galloped into the yard before swinging down from their horses and dashing inside the building. Seaton knew what to expect and, drawing his horse to a quick stop, flung himself clear of the saddle as shots began to ring out from inside the ranch-house. Taking advantage of whatever cover presented itself, he worked his way towards the building, returning fire as he did so. His attention was fixed on what was happening in front of him so that he didn't notice the presence of another gunman till the man was almost upon him. The cracking of a twig alerted him and he spun round, firing as he did so. The man staggered back, simultaneously firing his own gun. The bullet flew over Seaton's shoulder and the man turned and began to run. Seaton took a step to follow him when he felt a sharp pain in his upper arm. Blood seeped through but it wasn't his gun arm. Taken by surprise, he turned to see the marshal standing just inside the open doorway of the ranch-house with a rifle raised to his shoulder. A voice yelled, 'Get him, Braithwaite!'

Immediately Seaton dropped to the ground as the marshal fired. Bullets whistled just over his head as he hit the dirt, jarring his injured shoulder. He knew his position was desperate. Rolling to one side, he looked up. Braithwaite was partly concealed by the doorframe and didn't offer much of a target, but Seaton knew his bullet had to count. Taking just a moment to take aim, he pressed the trigger of his six-gun. There was a loud scream and Braithwaite spun round. He attempted to raise the rifle once more but Seaton was too quick and his second shot sent the marshal to the floor where he lay in a pool of blood, not moving. Seaton glanced about but there was no sign of the gunman who had fled and in a few moments the sound of hoof beats told him the man had made his escape. That left Brandon.

Getting to his feet, Seaton began to run towards the ranch-house, ducking and weaving as he went. Gunfire burst from inside the building, tearing up the dirt of the yard. He reached the porch steps and dashed up them, stepping over Braithwaite's body to enter the room. A quick glance told him that Brandon was not there. He looked towards the back of the room. A door stood open. Quickly he stepped forwards but even as he did so he heard a scream and Brandon appeared in the doorframe holding Maisie in front of him, with his arm around her neck and a revolver at her back.

'Drop the gun!' he hissed. Seaton hesitated for just a moment.

'I said drop the gun or the lady gets it!'

Seaton looked into Maisie's frightened eyes before letting his Colt fall to the floor. Pushing Maisie in front of him, Brandon stepped forward a pace.

'Who are you?' he said. Seaton did not reply.

'You've caused me an awful lot of trouble. I want to know who you are before I kill you.'

'Let Maisie go,' Seaton replied, 'and I'll tell you.'

Brandon gave an ugly laugh. 'Maisie,' he said. 'So it's Maisie, is it?' His face contorted. 'I'd say it was Miss Montgomery to you.'

'Leave Miss Montgomery alone. She has nothing to do with this.'

By way of reply, Brandon suddenly forced Maisie's head round and kissed her savagely. As she broke away, her lip bleeding, he broke into a laugh again.

'Once I've killed you, I'll deal with Miss Maisie,' he hissed.

With a sudden movement, he pushed her aside and levelled his gun at Seaton's chest.

'One more time,' he said. 'Who are you and what business do you have with me?'

'Unfinished business,' Seaton snapped. He allowed his eyes to stray beyond Brandon. 'Before you think of doin' anything else, I suggest you take a look behind you.'

Brandon's features creased in an ugly leer. 'Is that the best you can do?' he snarled.

He stepped forward a pace and, raising the gun, waved it in front Seaton's face.

'Goodbye, whoever you are,' he said.

He stared at Seaton with an evil intensity as his finger began to close on the trigger. Seaton tried to brace himself when suddenly the expression on Brandon's face changed. The evil leer was replaced by a look of surprise combined with pain. His eyes seemed to glaze over and the gun fell from his hand, striking the floor with a loud clatter. A wisp of blood appeared at the corner of his mouth and he opened his lips as if he was about to ask one more question. He swayed and Seaton stepped nimbly aside as he sank forward, striking his head against the wall as he fell. Protruding from his back was a long slim blade. Seaton looked up at the doorway where he had pretended that someone was standing behind Brandon. That old trick was a desperate ploy and he knew it wouldn't work. But now someone was there. Framed in the doorway was the worn figure of Utah.

'I saw you light out,' he said. 'Looks like I got here in the nick of time.' As the oldster stepped into the room, Seaton let out a huge sigh of relief.

'Sorry about the theatricals,' Utah said. 'Truth of the matter, after that fight with Brandon's boys, I was clean out of ammunition.'

Seaton opened his mouth to respond, but he had no chance because Maisie was already sobbing on his shoulder and his arms were wrapped tightly around her.

A couple of days had passed and Seaton and Utah were sitting by the campfire relaxing. A soft breeze rustled the leaves and blew some scraps of cloud among the stars. Utah finished off his mug of coffee and reached over to refill it.

'Seems like a long time since we were here,' he said.

'It only seems that way,' Seaton replied. 'A lot has happened since then.'

The oldster grinned and nodded his grizzled head. 'It sure has,' he said, 'but it's all turned out for the best.'

'We struck lucky,' Seaton responded. 'I have to admit there was a time there when I thought we'd taken on more than we could handle.'

'How's that wound?' Utah asked, looking at Seaton's bandaged arm.

'It's not much more than a graze.'

'I'd say it was more than that, but Miss Maisie sure did a good job of treatin' it.'

'With everythin' that happened, I barely noticed I'd been hit.'

Utah looked outside the circle of the fire at the looming shapes of the surrounding hills.

'Sure feels good to be back,' he mused.

'You figure you'll take up Montgomery's offer?' Seaton said.

'I reckon so. I ain't likely to get a better one.' Seaton thought he could detect a slight hesitancy in the oldster's voice and thought he knew the reason why.

'You'll see,' he said. 'Those sheep will be OK.'

'There weren't too many of 'em still alive, thanks to Brandon's gunslicks.'

'We'll round up the ones that are left and Montgomery will add to the flock. He's not askin' you to take charge of 'em as some kind of favour. As far as he's concerned it's a business proposition. If he had his way, he would have taken on Brownlow too, but it seems that he's had enough of the sheep business, at least around these parts.'

The oldster turned to Seaton with a twinkle in his eye. 'I guess he ain't got reason to stay on at the Lazy Ladder like you and me,' he said.

Seaton grinned. He knew Utah was referring to Maisie Montgomery but he didn't rise to the bait.

'He won't be needed to testify, that's for sure,' he replied. 'And as far as the Lazy Ladder is concerned, there's plenty of work to be done gettin' the place back on its feet, startin' as soon as I get back with roundin' up those beeves and trailin' 'em to the nearest rail head.'

The oldster took another drink of coffee.

'You're right there,' he said, 'neither of those two varmints are goin' to cause any more trouble. They deserved everythin' they got.'

'They're dead and gone,' Seaton said, 'it's time to forget 'em and look forward. Once the town meeting takes place, Lindenberg will have a proper marshal and things will be different.'

'It's just a pity that they took some good men with them,' Utah mused.

His words caused them to lapse into silence, each man thinking his own thoughts, till Utah broke the spell by getting to his feet and walking over to the horses. Seaton watched him, reflecting that his limp seemed almost to have gone, while he rummaged among his saddle-bags. In a moment or two he returned carrying something in his hand.

'Here,' he said, handing it to Seaton. Seaton took it, recognizing the pouch containing gold dust he had given the old man.

'Look on it as somethin' towards the future,' Utah said. 'I reckon you're gonna need it more than me.'